Deadbeat
DOGS OF WAUGH

DEADBEAT:
DOGS OF WAUGH

BY

GUY ADAMS

HUMDRUMMING LTD.,
Registered Offices: 8 Henley Street
Stratford-upon-Avon, Warwickshire
CV37 6PT, ENGLAND

This Paperback First Edition 2007

ISBN 978-1-905532-14-8

Cover designed by Guy Adams from a design
originally conceived by Lee Thompson

Prepared for publication by Ian Alexander Martin

First published by Humdrumming, 2007
www.humdrumming.co.uk
ISBN 978-1-905532-14-8

© This book is printed on paper made
from fully managed and sustained
forest sources.

FSC

Printed and bound in
the United Kingdom
by Biddles Ltd.

TT-COC-002303

© 1996 Forest Stewardship Council A.C.

Dedicated to Mattie

pre-titles

After hours, and the traffic lights bleed onto wet tarmac. Neon bounces reflections everywhere you turn and somewhere in the distance drunks laugh at the jiggle of cellulite buttocks sliced through by glitter spandex. This isn't the hustle and bustle of daylight hours: this is the flip-side, the kingdom of shadows which comes out to play when the streetlamps begin to glow. The wolves hunt on street corners, guzzling their cans of lager and whistling at hookers; the lost and wounded huddle in doorways, praying for just one more dawn; and bleary eyed taxi drivers tune-out to drive-time hoping for the one more fare that'll get them the hell out of there.

Yes, that's right, it's me: Max Jackson, Suburban Poet and Habitual Barfly, lost in the backstreets of Soho and high as a hamster in a snow pile of crack.

I do seem to get myself in some pickles don't I?

In fact I'm thinking of having my name changed to "Max Pickles" just to simplify matters. Or maybe "Pickles Jackson", what do you think?

Nah… sounds like a black comedy character in an old movie. I'd grow tired rolling my eyes and gurning all the time.

Yus Massuh!

Forgive me, not thinking straight at the moment.

Pulse racing, I can hear my heart thudding in my ears, sweat pouring off me. Every part of me is twitching, every nerve, every muscle, *every bloody hair follicle*. I want to be sick, but there's nothing to throw up. Besides I haven't the time, because I can hear it behind me and it's gaining. I don't know where I'm running to; I have no plan of action: this is basic 'fight or flight' stuff.

And 'fight' really isn't an option.

Trust me.

"Excuse me, pal."

Shit…

He shuffles in front of me, stained blanket 'round his shoulders and the dregs of a Special Brew in his pink and chapped fist.

"Spare some change, mate?"

Not now! I haven't got the time or energy. I move to run past him but he follows and we're dancing like footballers.

"C'mon pal, just a couple of quid for god's sake!"

He's getting angry and — looking into his dilated eyes — I realise I'm face to face with a brother space cadet, so there'll be no space for reason in our negotiations. My trip was force-fed, but this guy's got a monkey on his back the size of King Kong and I just bet it's horny for a banana.

"Out of the way!" I shout and make to shove him to one side. Which, considering his mental state, is something of a mistake. He screams at me and clouts the side of my head with his fist. That's all it takes to knock what little physical control I have into touch: I'm on my arse in the gutter within seconds, with no clear idea of how I could ever get back up again.

Then I see it.

He'd called it a "dog" — the bastard who had set it on me in the first place — but, drug addled brain or not, I couldn't quite accept the description. There was a touch of the canine to it sure enough, but only enough to highlight quite how *un*-dog-like the rest of it was. If a rabid buffalo had decided to go to a fancy dress party in dog disguise, then this was how I imagine it would look as it loitered by the canapés waiting to strike. A sinewy ripple of muscle and teeth, froth at the mouth, and nothing you could relate to in the eyes. If their owner had given it exercise, I imagine it would be more likely located in a war zone than a park.

"All I wanted was a couple of quid!" the addict shouts, completely blind to the creature that is standing no more than a few feet away from him. I'd got used to that by now; there was something about these beasts that just slipped off the eyes. Maybe they were just too much for a rational mind to take, or maybe there was some kind of hocus-pocus going on. Whichever it was, when these things ran free on the night time streets, nobody seemed to notice but me.

The homeless guy could certainly feel it though. I could tell that by the short scream he gave as it pounced on him and gently tore off his face; a wet tearing sound like Velcro. Then the beast turns — with fresh meat hanging from its mouth — to look at me.

DEADBEAT:
DOGS OF WAUGH

max

1.

I'm famous for many things of course. Accepted, they're not your run-of-the-mill achievements, nobody's going to put my face on any stamp or pound note in the near future. Still, tell me who else you know that can quote *Withnail & I* line for line, or eat an entire packet of Fisherman's Friends *in one mouthful* without throwing up? Who else do you know that can skid over twenty feet, using nothing more than a velvet cushion and a polished wooden dance floor? Regularly? Who else do you know that has drunk an entire bottle of imported Vodka from the bell of a trombone? A-ha! That's right people: it's a short list.

With skills like these it's no great surprise that I luxuriate in the company of several high class Homo Sapiens. Take Tom Harris for instance, a five-and-a-half-foot (plus loose change) love predator and jazz freak he may be, but he owns his own nightclub and has rubbed shoulders with the likes of Olivier, Guilgud and Schofield (though, granted, this was because he worked in the Bar of the Royal Shakespeare Theatre in his youth, not because he met them professionally; theatre director he may have been, but there are levels in every community and he operated on the more subterranean strata of the boards — which was where he met me, of course.).

It's Tom's nightclub that I do most of my drinking in, mainly because it's a classy joint — and I am nothing if not a man of discerning tastes — but also because the drinks were free and he hires bar staff with cracking tits. Sadly he also employs a manager by the name of Len Horowitz, who sees it as his life's mission to keep me from both booze and bosom as frequently as possible. Bastard. As dry as a Camel's Martini, Len was a good manager and possessor of the best Walrus moustache I've ever seen. I'd still have given him a good slap had I dared, but he'd only have set the security staff on me and they're a handy bunch of lads, most particularly when it came to the kicking-in of heads.

"Watch what you're doin' you soft wee frigger!" shouted Douggie, head of security and last year's winner of the Most Red Haired Highland Butch Homo Award (by default I believe, the nominations were few and Douggie scared them all away come award night).

I stood next to Chas and Dave — his fellow bouncers that night — and laughed like a loon while looking around the busy club to see if I could spot who it was that had wound Douggie up.

It's embarrassing in hindsight, but meant little to me at the time, that it was only when I felt Dave's slightly cold hand on my shoulder and heard him shout in my ear that I realised it was *me*.

"I'd get out of his way, Mr. Jackson. Douggie's not in a good way this evening. Steve taped over his copy of the Boy George *A-Team* episode and he's looking to take it out on someone."

Steve lives with Douggie and does something in computers. We're assuming he does something in Douggie as well, but they keep that quiet.

Chas and Dave are good blokes, simple of course, you'd have to be to walk around calling yourselves "Chas and Dave" (their given names, but still: after a few years of "Rabbit Rabbit" wherever you went, you'd change it, wouldn't you? Surely? Perhaps they like the fights it frequently helps to start).

I like to think I said:

"Fair enough boys, I quite understand, have a good night."

However, it's reported that I screamed:

"I ain't getting on no plane!" and ran into the crowd.

That will have been the import Vodka I believe.

The band was particularly good that night, but then I was biased as they were backing a new singer Tom had booked a few times and I had taken something of a shine to her. Called herself Debruvio, which sounded a lot more foreign than *she* did but it looked classy on the posters. We got on ever so well. Sparkled, y'know? Wit and flirtation, lots of laughter.

Well, that's the way it was in my head.

In actuality, we'd never spoken. I was building up to it, biding my time, playing it cool, hoping to impress with my *savoir faire*…

Tonight that included running up and down in front of the stage with a large floor cushion on my head screaming "Tam O'Shanter!" repeatedly.

That will have been the import Vodka, I believe. Again.

I was having a little bit of a rest in one of the decorative pot plants, when I noticed a guy out of the corner of my eye behaving weirdly. Big feller with a nice suit and tie; liked his cake and could afford to buy plenty. He was sat at a corner table, a young woman next to him looking bored, gazing into space and, occasionally, the eyes of the Tenor Sax player.

He was sweating, *a lot*: the front of his shirt turned grey with the wet, clinging to his chest and gut. Both hands were on the table, palms down, shaking. As I watched the shaking got worse, building up along his arms and through into the rest of his body. His girl finally noticed once he started thrashing back against the padded bench seat, his fists hammering into the glass table enough to make it crack.

She tugged at him, trying to loosen his tie and shirt collar, and began shouting for help. A couple at the next table moved over to help — although they didn't seem to have a clue as to how to accomplish that — and then the whole thing turned just plain nasty.

The fat man screamed and gave his girlfriend a savage punch under the chin, she fell backwards with a broken jaw and a startled look, while the other couple backed away deciding — perfectly sensibly — that he might be about to turn on them next.

The man got to his feet and roared, only the tables closest to him noticing as Debruvio and the band were hammering out the high note of "Fever" at the time.

A couple of guys tried to get him under control, jumping on a shoulder each and throwing their weight into it, hoping to bring him down. Whatever fit was coursing through his system had given him some pep though, as he screamed and knocked one of them backwards while throwing the other over his shoulder and into a Hen Night party — I'd spent five drunken minutes trying to convince the bride-to-be of her dreadful error earlier, and had managed to earn a kiss and a fluffy pink tiara from the Maid of Honour on the strength of my argument.

The rest of the drinkers began to notice — that Mexican-wave ripple of information that always happens in a busy club when a fight breaks out — and one by one heads turned and people began to rise from their seats. The band, being old pros, played on and I saw Chas and Dave making their way as quickly as men of their size can towards the situation. I'd been intending to step in, obviously, but as the professionals were getting involved I thought I might be better placed in a supporting role and adopted a position of covering fire from behind my rubber plant.

"Evening, Dearest," Tom said, as he sidled in next to me, while passing me a freshly mixed Caiprinha. "Quiet night?"

"Yeah…" I took a sip: crushed ice, lime and a kick like a Brazilian Hooker. Beautiful. "The horn section wants me to pay for a new trombone, the singer is still unaware of how much she wants to sleep with me, Douggie's out for blood, and a fat man broke your table."

"What's got Douggie's back up?"

"Steve taped over his *A-Team*."

"Not the Boy George episode?"

"Yep."

"Oh dear… handbags at dawn."

We both ducked as a chair flew past us.

Chas and Dave were doing fine, but the guy was a match for their size; purple face, spit and punches flying. They were spending more time trying to avoid his blows than they were getting their own in. Back-up was on its way though, Douggie striding towards them with a clenched teeth smile.

"I'll deal with one of your horn problems." Tom said, "But the other's up to you."

"Thanks mate." Tom was cool like that.

Douggie walked right up to the man and slammed a fist into his nose.

"I pity the foo'!" he shouted. The man toppled backwards, crashed to the floor and stayed there. Douggie walked off, calm for the first time that evening.

The band dusted down Gershwin's "Summertime" and Debruvio sang a D minor that made my heart and trousers soar.

"That's that then." Tom said and we both got out from behind the plant pot. "Let's see if he paid his bill."

"And find out what made him flip of course." I suggested.

"First things first, old Love; first things first."

2.

The news was doubly bad.

First of all, he'd possessed a taste for some particularly fine champagne and brandy and had flipped with a bar tab that had already crept over the ton. Add to that the damage and a free round of drinks for those directly in the line of fire and Arbuckle was into Tom for a fair few quid. This in itself would have been no great hardship were it not for the second piece of bad news: he was dead.

Now, let me be specific here, sheer lack of what the science world thinks of as 'life' is no great problem amongst the *clientèle* of Deadbeat; it did cater, after all, to that rather small subculture of folk who had known a little fatality in their existence. Tom, Dave, myself... Hell, well over half of the customers currently tapping a foot and raising a glass in the building have more familiarity with death than is customary. This guy though was DEAD dead. You could tell by looking at him that he had been reanimated — there is something to the skin colour, wrongness to the eyes, 'takes one to know one kind of thing', you know? — but he had died AGAIN. This time it seemed to be a permanent state. Which just DOESN'T HAPPEN. When you come back you stay that way. It is, frankly, one of the drawbacks to the condition.

And if you don't see that as a drawback then fuck you, I could introduce you to a number of old timers whose bodies have begun to pack up in some major and unsightly ways who would put you straight. I've got some sticky years ahead of me, okay?

We try not to think about it.

Christ, I need a drink.

So, Tubs was walking dead. But something had KILLED him. Creepy.

Tom had the bouncers carry the body into his office and put in a call to Thackeray.

3.

While we waited for Thackeray and his medical ways, I sat down at the bar and tried to calm myself. I was sobering up quickly now, freaked by stuff I didn't understand and reminded of stuff I liked to forget. Joe, one of the bar staff — a young lad with too much hair, earrings and rock in his soul for Tom's liking — recognised my mood and quickly poured a drink.

I stared at it for awhile, watching the spot lighting of the bar bounce around in the crushed ice. Breathing slow, making myself calm and centred. Barfly Voodoo.

I was just about there, when I felt someone come and stand next to me; a waft of Chanel and the rustle of a cocktail dress. Debruvio.

I wasn't ready for this, wasn't feeling confident enough. Still… I'd be saying that for the next few years knowing me and, besides, she could only say 'no'.

I opened my mouth to speak.

"Fuck off, cushion boy", she muttered and took her Gin and Tonic away to where the band was sitting.

Nice.

I waved Joe over.

"Fetch me an ice pick would you? I would very much like to gouge my eyes out now."

4.

Thackeray arrived at just gone midnight, looking every inch the country gent, head to foot tweed and a mustard waistcoat covered in cat hair. Likes his cats, does Thackeray.

"Thanks for coming Jeffrey", Tom said, shaking him by the hand. "He's in my office."

"It says so much about you that I didn't realise you possessed one", Thackeray replied with a smile. "You seem to make all of your decisions from a barstool."

"True, true, but it's a bugger for the paperwork, you can only fit so many invoices in a pint pot. Len converted me to the notion of a separate room to rejoice in the wonders of a filing cabinet."

"Now all he has to do is learn how to work one", I added as we walked out the back.

Tom's office is actually very nice — a fact certainly helped by the lack of time he spends in it — a large, dark, wood desk offers some degree of work ethic, but it's the leather sofas that make the place comfy. The walls are filled with autographed photos of his jazz heroes: Gillespie, Ellington, Coltrane… A pricey Bang and Olufsen turntable sits ready and waiting to spin something from Tom's beloved vinyl collection. He even has a couple of pot plants.

Of course, the dead fat guy in the middle of the floor was fucking with the Feng Shui right then, but hopefully things would be back to normal soon.

Thackeray dropped to his haunches and gave the man a brisk examination. "I doubt I'll be able to tell anything without taking a blood sample, though I have to say I don't hold out much hope."

"Hardly Quincy is he?" I muttered. Tom nudged me in the ribs with his elbow.

"Why, old chap?" he asked.

" I've already seen a couple of other people turn up like this and, as it's so damned unheard of, I've been looking into it as a result. I haven't been able to turn up much so far, though." He looked up at us both. "We've all had our allotted go with Death; it goes against what little we know about the condition when one of us has *another* crack at it."

"Go back a minute," I said. "You're saying this isn't the first time this has happened?"

"No. The first was a couple of weeks ago: a man was found floating down-river; caused a bit of upset amongst a bunch of Japanese tourists who were trying to photograph Tower Bridge at the time. Police fished him out and decided — from his clothing, the state of the body, and the lack of any visible attack wounds — that he was a drunken party-goer who had fallen in some time ago, only to reappear when the gases in his body forced him back up. It happens. I've seen my fair share of bloated floaters."

"Clothing?" Tom asked.

"Breeches, stockings and an embroidered frock coat, rather ostentatious nowadays. A friend of mine contacted me when they brought him in to Pathology. I was able to get down there and arrange a convenient hush job. The body was burned and nobody wiser. I didn't feel it would do any of us any favours to have the authorities carving away at a Nineteenth Century Earl of my occasional acquaintance."

"You've a friend in 'the Met' then?" said Tom, with a smile.

"Oh, I've got friends *everywhere*. I wouldn't have access to half of the materials I have otherwise."

"What about the second fellah?" I asked.

"Much less public, thankfully, if a little sad." He looked at Tom. "You remember James Pullman?"

Tom nodded. "He played piano here once or twice, nice man. Never really took to his new life though, didn't make friends easily, bit morose, but a good heart."

"Not anymore: it virtually exploded in his chest last Thursday. As you say he didn't really know anybody. He could have been there in his flat for months before anyone found him. As it was, I've been treating him — bad skin patches, dryness, and poor renewal of skin cells — so had popped 'round to give him some new oil. Poor man was in the middle of the floor, limbs contracted, face contorted. Clearly not a peaceful last few minutes."

"That rings a few bells", Tom muttered, sitting down on one of the sofas. "You didn't think to mention this to anyone?"

"Of course not! The last thing I wanted was to cause a lot of panic when I didn't have the first idea what was happening. It's clearly some form of seizure, but as to what causes it…?" He sighed, then stared at the photograph of Beiderbecke on Tom's wall for a moment, his thoughts elsewhere. "Sorry," he said eventually, "ignorance is a cancer to an inquiring mind. Do you want me to dispose of the body?"

"I'll have one of the boys do it," Tom replied, "you have enough on your plate. If you need anything, you just have to ask: you know that, don't you, Jeffrey?"

Thackeray smiled. "Thank you, old man. Let's just hope we can sort this out without stirring up even more trouble, shall we?"

"Fat chance of that in my experience," I mumbled opening the door to the office, "we'll be knee deep in chaos by this time tomorrow; 'tis the Harris / Jackson way."

Thackeray sighed, "Oh for a quiet life."

"When it goes on forever?" Tom laughed. "My dear Jeremy, where would be the fun in that?"

5.

It's a magical time in the nightclub business, that sudden hush that follows the last drunken stumbles back onto the street and the final clunk of the lock being turned. It's not dissimilar to the theatre, post-show: house lights up, actors milling about in their normal clothes looking for that last nightcap and return to normality, before tomorrow night swings 'round and the fantasy begins again. The magic stripped, bright light and the sweeping up of fag ends and the mopping of spilled booze.

I don't see it often (I'm either being swept around with the fag ends, or face down on one of the sofas), but sat at the bar with a large cappuccino and a mind that was coming to terms with sobriety, I made a mental note to catch it again sometime. It was rather relaxing.

"What do you think?" asked Tom for what was maybe the sixth or seventh time.

"I don't know…" I said. AGAIN.

"There's really only one thing I care about", Len said. We'd already filled him in on everything Thackeray had told us. "Do I own this place if you two peg it?"

"I intend to have you buried with me like the ancient Egyptians and their cats; I couldn't possibly manage on the other side without you", Tom said with a smile.

"Hmm… As tempting as it might be to watch you blaze in hell-fire for eternity, my own sufferings would probably be a distraction. I'd best help to solve this in any way I can," he sipped his drink, "the status quo being the best chance I appear to have for contentment."

"How depressing for you", I said, rubbing stray milk froth from my nose.

"My life may as well be over. Have you considered talking to Jerusalem?"

Tom and I looked at one another.

"Which way are you supposed to face?" Tom smirked.

"Mecca's that way," I answered pointing to the band stage.

"*Danny* Jerusalem, you blithering idiots. Christ, it's hard work; I may as well call the Krankies and see if they want to help."

"Do you want to sit on my knee?" I asked Tom.

"Later, perhaps. Who's 'Danny Jerusalem'?"

"Shady little sod, deals in magic and occult stuff, I wouldn't trust him an inch but from what I hear he knows his subject."

"You're suggesting we go the 'Alternative Therapy' route?" I said.

"Well, if Thackeray's stumped, I can't see the harm. What's the worst that can happen?"

"We can always pick some stuff up while we're there," I suggested. "Eye of Newt? Bum of Frog? Y'know: see if he can cure your bald patch, maybe."

"Or your verbal diarrhoea", Len countered

"Where does he trade from?" Tom interjected, hoping to stop the pair of us before we began fighting playground style.

"A pub just off The Strand called 'The Deveraux'."

6.

Accepting that little could be done for now, Tom and I went our separate ways agreeing to make a trip across town tomorrow evening.

My flat isn't the most luxurious of real estate, a one-bedroom box of mildew and nicotine-stained wallpaper which I share with a number of verminous tenants — of both the furred and the carapaced variety. It's directly above a kebab shop which I'm assuming adds to the critter appeal; I once caught a small rat licking fat juice from the skirting boards. I'm hoping cardiac problems will deal with the bastard so I don't have to. One particularly drunk and paranoid evening, I found myself rubbing lard into the stair-carpet in an attempt to hasten matters. I need taking in hand, I really do.

I made myself a coffee — strange as it may seem, I wasn't in the mood for booze anymore — put a David Bowie CD on and settled down in front of my computer.

People always seem surprised that I own one. I obviously give off a Luddite air or something. Of course I have a computer: you can't access the internet without one and the internet is the lifeblood of any single man. It feeds me DVDs, illegal downloads, books, and heroic quantities of hardcore porn.

I have hobbies. Some of them you just wouldn't do in company that's all.

Well… *polite* company anyway.

I tooled around for awhile — in that wonderfully vacuous, time-stealing way the internet has — looking at news pages, following links, consuming nonsense in an etheric paper-trail.

I wasn't really in the mood for sleep.

I do DO it.

Sleep that is.

People ask; they seem to think that, being reanimate, I would have given up the habit or something. It's true that I don't need as much as I used to but, obviously, I still need *some*. Nothing can survive entirely without sleep. Not just for the purposes of rest either, I remember reading once that we sleep to dream, that without dreaming we would go insane. When dreaming the human mind can let go, unhinge safely while we're out for the count and are unlikely to damage ourselves. The night is filled with quiet lunatics, tired after a day of having to be sane, all going bug-shit for awhile, because otherwise they would adopt the condition permanently.

What a species we are.

I had had enough crazy for one night.

Screw sleep; bring me porn.

You might want to step outside for a bit… unless you want to watch while…? No, I didn't think you looked the type.

7.

Tom called 'round about six and we hit The Tube.

There is an attitude — highly prevalent amongst those lucky enough to live outside London — that the Underground is 'a cool thing'. An exciting and atmospheric place. As a kid I always felt the same, loving the tiled tunnels and the rush of air on the platform as a train crept close. It was a world of echoing busker magic and the smell of worn rubber.

I hate it now. It's a place of push-me pull-you and get-the-fuck-out-of-my-way. It serves a purpose — it does get you from A to B — just don't expect me to like it. The fact that my attitude changed so quickly once moving to London makes me hate it all the more. Another bastard that didn't live up to my childish dreams.

On the Northern line to Embankment, then jump a stop on the District, then to Temple. Tom and I emerge into the world of lawyers and stately brick, the Thames at our backs.

The one thing London is very good at is variety, and the Underground can help with that as it robs your journey of transition. You keep emerging in conflicting areas with only the fact that your map tells you you're in the same city to prove you haven't jumped towns. Like Enid Blyton's 'Faraway Tree', you never know what world could be at the top of the Underground tunnels.

The Deveraux is pretty well hidden at the bottom of a lane just beyond the Justice Buildings.

Inside it's all dark wood and deep red carpet, traditional pub chic with the walls painted a clotted cream to hide the stain of pipe and cigarette smoke.

We asked after Jerusalem at the bar, but the Czech girl shook her head;

although due to not knowing him or not understanding, we couldn't quite tell.

Sitting down at a corner table, taking a high-backed settle each, Tom and I sipped at our pints, sizing the other customers up as we looked around and kept any eye on the door for new people arriving.

Which was ridiculous of course, as we had no idea what he looked like. Unless Danny Jerusalem was kind enough to walk in sporting a voodoo face mask, covered head-to-toe in brightly coloured feathers, it was unlikely we were going to peg him on sight. I mentioned as much to Tom.

"Good point. We have gone about this in a rather half-cocked manner."

"Max Jackson and Tom Harris: The Demi-Cock Detectives."

"Catchy. All we can do is ask around until someone tells us how to find him. If nothing else, he'll probably get to hear that we're looking. He might end-up finding us."

"What for? To shrink our bloody heads?"

"Excuse me?"

"You know: 'shrunken heads on belts', 'witch-doctor shit'. He'll probably keep our souls in bottles or something."

"Don't be ridiculous! You don't even believe in that sort of thing."

"Nobody does, until they're about to meet someone who might do it for a hobby. Do you think he'll stick pins in dolls of us, 'to teach us the folly of our unbelieving ways'?"

"Dear Christ, Max, we only want to ask him a few things, your imagination is a terrible handicap sometimes."

"So is having no head." I picked up my beer mat and started tearing around the edges to form a cross shape that I hoped might protect me against devilry should the chips not fall our way.

"Or just not using the one you've got", said the man that had been sat next to me ever since I'd arrived. I'd always known he was there, but somehow hadn't been able to think about the fact. I could see him, feel the weight of him on the settle, I just couldn't *care*. As if he was just part of the furniture.

Danny Jerusalem is a clever sod. I'll give him that.

"You wanted me? You've got me. Mine's a Scotch and Coke. Double."

8.

Aside from his ability to not be noticed — as much a psychological trick as a magical one, he claimed — there was little eerie or weird about Danny Jerusalem. In fact I found myself more able to imagine him selling me a used car than an incantation. There was a rough, unfriendly aspect to him: he made no effort to be pleasant to either of us. But I suppose in his line of work he doesn't have to: people come to him when they want what he can offer. It's a seller's market in the spells and charms game. He dressed like a mechanic on a night out, tatty jeans and a leather jacket, threadbare at the edges and rife with the fug of a thousand smoked cigarettes.

Tom explained what we had seen in the bar, and Jerusalem just nodded for awhile then suddenly held up his hand. "Leave it there, we'll talk more somewhere else."

Again, without an ounce of social grace, he stood up and urged us out of the pub and onto the street.

"You sound like you know what's going on", Tom said as we marched to keep up with him.

"You're in a different world here, boys. Outside your comfortable little zombie niche, your cocktails and cabaret. Keep your gob shut until we're off the street."

Tom raised an eyebrow towards me — at Jerusalem's manner in general as well as his use of the 'z' word — but stayed silent as we followed Jerusalem through a criss-cross of side-streets until we stood at a plain door between a second-hand bookshop and a computer repair place. Danny unlocked the door and gestured for us to go in.

Up a small flight of stairs to the first floor and we were in Danny's flat: a little more modern and minimalist than I would have given him credit for, with lots of chrome and glass. Tom dropped down onto a leather sofa and struggled to maintain his dignity a little as the soft cushion had him sinking down and bringing his feet up off the floor. "How relaxing," he sighed, "furniture you can get lost in."

Danny ignored him, walking over to a sideboard where he slid a CD from its rack and placed it in the player next to it. He pressed PLAY and then strolled into the open kitchen, pouring us all a drink from an icy bottle of Stolichnaya he pulled out of the freezer.

"Catchy tune." I said. The CD was playing, but the speakers sat in complete silence.

"You may not be able to dance to it, but it's perfect for background music." He smiled for the first time, and placed our drinks on the coffee table before taking a seat in the armchair facing us. "It's one of a collection I picked up in Bulgaria, a whole range of auditory spells. I have CDs here that would make you excessively open to suggestion, paralyse you from head to toe, or just knock you unconscious within seconds of pressing PLAY."

'Oh yeah?' I said, 'I'm like that with *Wet Wet Wet*; what's this one then?'

'It's the magical equivalent of white noise: outside the few square feet where we're sitting, nobody can hear a word we're saying, whether via the naked ear, microphone or... more esoteric methods. We can say what we like now without worrying about eavesdroppers."

"Should we have been worrying about it before then?" Tom gave a half-smile and I could tell he was writing Jerusalem off as either a show-off or a paranoid. Jerusalem obviously picked up on it.

"As I said, you're a long way from your usual haunts, you have no idea how things work here amongst the living."

"I think you write us off a little easily", Tom replied, sipping at his vodka, thick and smooth.

"Maybe, but as I know exactly what's affecting your *clientèle*... and *how* it is, you'll forgive the assumption. Your *naïveté* proves my point, rather."

"So enlighten us."

"I intend to, but my point of you moving in a different circle is a valid one. Society likes its ghettoes... for all of humanity's talk of 'unity' and 'equality' we section ourselves off into comfortable cliques the first opportunity we get. You two have more cause than most..."

"The rest of society wouldn't exactly embrace us with open arms", I agreed.

"No, it wouldn't and your need for secrecy is the greatest weapon anyone has against you.

"You're being targeted as a niche market, and frankly that's why I'm talking to you. Your problem goes by the name of Auberon Waugh, a small time pusher with aspirations."

"Sounds more like a flouncy poet", I chuckled, taking another sip of my Vodka and hoping for a top-up.

"Looks like one too, but he sees himself more as a new age Aleister Crowley, a hard-on for magic and sufficient immorality to cut corners. He works a similar line to me..."

"Spell pusher..." Tom muttered with a degree of distaste.

Jerusalem looked him straight in the eye. "How nice it must be to feel that secure cynicism. We all earn a living, old man, some of us even do so with a sense of principle."

"Where do reanimates fit in then?" I asked quickly, determined not to let this descend into an argument.

"Waugh has isolated a substance that gives the living dead the experience of life. It allows you to feel the blood running again in your veins, your heart rate pounding, your respiration going through the roof."

"Sounds delightful." Tom said.

"I know as well as you do that it's an attractive prospect to many of you. It's a hard existence to come to terms with."

"True." Tom stared at his drink and I could tell he was thinking of poor James Pullman, the piano player Thackeray had found. "Point is... what are we supposed to do about it?" Tom said.

We sat in silence for a second as there really was no obvious answer to that.

Eventually, Jerusalem cheered us up even further: "You realise of course that this stuff isn't your only problem? You're threatening exposure. Either by more and more of you turning up in the public eye, or by those in Waugh's organisation talking. Right now it's small, a tiny outfit with a wish to get bigger. Soon, this stuff could be on sale from somewhere else." He finished his drink and slammed the glass on the table, theatrical bastard. "Or you could find your little society stamped out in a panicked witch hunt by people terrified of the very possibility of you."

9.

We were about to take our leave of Jerusalem's door when the sound of screeching metal made both Tom and I duck for cover. There had been little else to say frankly and, rather than sit being more and more doom-laden conversationally, we were eager to get back to the club and think all this through.

"What the fuck was that?" I shouted, the sound of a car alarm blaring from the main road around the corner.

"A crash?" Tom suggested.

Jerusalem rolled his eyes and began to jog in the direction of the noise, "Bloody thing..."

Tom and I looked at one another, somewhat bemused, before following.

When we turned onto the main road we were presented with a somewhat unusual sight: a Kia Rio — alarm blaring, lights flashing — slowly spinning on its roof in the middle of the road. There were no other cars in sight, nor did there appear to be any other damage to the car than a rather crumpled upper half where it rested on the ground.

"Is anyone hurt?" Tom shouted over the sound of the alarm.

"Nah... it was empty, they usually are." Jerusalem replied looking left and right as if he'd lost something.

"Never seen anything like it!" came a voice from up the street, a rather drunk old man was walking towards us, a small, black-and-white cat in his arms. He had the clothing and swagger that suggested he was heading back to his park bench for a good night's kip. "The car just lifted into the air, flipped over, and then dropped onto its roof!"

Tom started to laugh but the look on Jerusalem's face was dead straight as he said to the old man, ""

The guy looked at the animal in his arms which was busily purring and accepting the attention, "Yours, is it? Yeah… running like the clappers, weren't it? Scared by the noise I imagine, don't blame it."

The cat jumped from his arms and padded towards us. Jerusalem, clearly angry, gave a snarl and reached to pick it up. The cat side-stepped him neatly and came and sat by my ankles.

"Fucking thing will be the death of me," he muttered.

"Eat you out of house and home, don't they?" the old guy chuckled.

Jerusalem looked him in the eye. "Go away," he whispered.

The old man's face went blank, then he turned around and marched off in the opposite direction.

"Useful… you'll have to show my door staff that one," said Tom.

"Saves idiotic questions."

"Not from me it won't", I said. "What's with the cat then?"

Danny sighed and began to walk back towards his flat, a few more people were starting to gather around the car. One of them, by the way they were shouting and pointing at it, seemed a likely candidate for its owner.

"Long story… he was dumped on me by a supplier I worked with for awhile, mad guy who fancied himself some *Voudoun* big-shot from Haiti… 'Brixton Bill' we called him; silly bastard had never been further than Benidorm on a package deal. Knew his stuff though…' he nodded at the cat, 'reanimated this little feller after he'd found him by the side of the road. Some bastard had hit him with their car."

"He's a reanimate?" I said, immediately slightly embarrassed by how important that felt. I'd be wearing T-Shirts for reanimate rights next.

"Yeah…man-made though I suppose, which seems to have given him the odd… *kink.*"

"Like what?" Asked Tom.

Danny gestured his head towards the car behind us.

"He doesn't like cars much…"

Tom and I looked at one another.

"You saying *he* did that?" I said eventually.

"Best I can figure out; every few weeks he wanders off and next thing you know there's somebody's ride on its roof or in a ditch or — on one bloody freaky occasion — hanging from the tree in their front lawn."

"Right… doesn't like cars." I couldn't quite get my head around it. It seemed even more ridiculous than the rest of my day-to-day experiences (and those were *pretty* ridiculous generally).

I looked at the little guy, black and white with big eyes that spoke volumes of naughtiness.

I've always been a cat person. There's something about them, an attitude, a *quirkiness* that makes me feel at home with them. I rubbed behind his ears and smiled as he started purring. They always seem to like me too…

"I guess he picked up more than an extra life from the mad old witch doctor," Danny said.

"That makes it ten lives," Tom smiled. "Some would call that plain greedy. What's his name?"

Danny looked embarrassed, "Silly bastard called him *'Mattifilarius'*."
We laughed. "It's probably Latin for 'Sad, Pretentious Git' ", Tom
suggested.
"Yeah... I prefer Mattie."

10.

Danny gave us a small business card with his number on it and nothing
else (if you had one, you knew what he did and appreciated it was best
not placed in print), then Tom and I took our leave, walking back past
the upturned car — there were two policeman staring at it now, trying
to calm the owner who hadn't stopped shouting and thrashing his arms
around.

We managed to find our way back to the Tube station eventually after
a couple of wrong turns (one being into a little wine bar... damn, but we
had been sure it was a shortcut... the Sauvignon Blanc seemed to make it
take longer, if anything).

We talked on the way of course, it had been a night of Big Thoughts...
and, when considering what we were supposed to do about any of it (if,
indeed we should do anything at all) Big Questions.

"I for one don't see that there's much we *can* do about it", Tom said,
"though it pisses me off to roll over."

I knew what he meant of course: sticking our noses into people's
business was one thing, but squaring up to a drug dealer and his gang
wasn't exactly within our sphere of capabilities.

"Worth mentioning it to Thackeray though," I suggested, "and see if
any of his connections can do anything."

"True", Tom agreed. "Plus prep Doug and the boys to keep an eye for
any users on the door."

"Yeah..."

It left a sour taste, this acquiescence...

We passed through the ticket barrier and into the swimming pool-
tiled tunnel of Temple. Some old soak was hacking his way through "Hey
Jude" on the penny whistle and I aimed a coin in his direction; sadly
falling short of his throat and into his flat cap, heigh-ho...

We waited a few minutes on the platform, both lost in our own
thoughts... I watched a kid's silver balloon, half-deflated but caught in
the thermal air currents, bobbing in the mouth of the tunnel, flotsam
caught in the air stream...

Hoarding posters told me how to be flasher; richer, sexier... I ignored
them. They didn't know me and their advice was of little interest...

The air changed, the wind rushing ahead of the train sending the
balloon whipping crazily up towards the ceiling.

The train pulled up, thinly dressed with the last few late-night die-
hards who had enough change in their pockets to get them back home

again. The doors hissed open and Tom and I climbed in. Just as the warning began to beep and the recorded voice told us that the doors were closing, there was a flash of movement and, as the train made its way into the tunnel, I wondered quite how Mattie had managed to follow us all the way. How had he managed to pay for a ticket, for that matter?

The cat was smart.

waugh

1.

Oh to be in Paris, dallying amongst the bars and pavement cafés, nothing but the sound of pigeon's wings and gentle jazz in my ears. Or Marrakech perhaps? Not as sedate, not as peaceful, but at least the stimulations and amusements were varied and pleasurable...

Oh to be anywhere but here.

"So, Auberon, whattya think? Do we have a deal, or what?"

Dear Lord, but I could hear the English language crying out in pain with every word. The little turd's overly familiar use of my first name hadn't gone unnoticed either, but he had made such a habit of it since first stepping into my office that I had long since decided to let it pass. For now, certainly.

"Mr. Silkin," I crossed my legs and tried to maintain a degree of comfort in this most dreadful of company by resting my eyes on a couple of the lovely Beardsley prints that hung on the wall just behind him. He was a vulgar and tasteless man — Silkin of course, never Mr. Beardsley; he had tastes aplenty and I shared them — squaddie hair and a suit that could only have come off a high-street peg. "Let me just make sure we understand one another perfectly. You feel that I am treading on your... 'turf' somewhat with these little business interests of mine..."

"You know you are, let's not piss about here! Your men are all over my streets and that's not how things are done..."

"Please," said I, as I held up my — oh-so-soft and perfectly turned — hand. "I'm just summing up the situation... in return for this trespass — and by way of a gentleman's apology — you wish to receive sixty percent of my revenue or you will be forced to take preventative measures."

Silkin smiled. " 'Preventative measures'... I like that. Basically, yeah, you should have come to me in the first place... a mistake, but I'm a reasonable bloke and I'm sure we can work this out without resorting to..." he rolled the word around in his mouth, like a fat schoolboy with a sweetie, " 'preventative measures'. Sixty percent is fair, and a better price than the alternative."

I sighed, now the little oik was dishing out veiled threats again, I do so *hate* veiled threats, only the weak need ever use them.

"I see." I glanced over at Silkin's colleague: a fellow called Aycliffe, no doubt present to make me feel uncomfortable — something which it failed to do, given that the young man had a fair appearance and considerably more sense than his employer — with his hands away from his weapon which was no doubt concealed under his jacket, and eyes turned to the window where he seemed more interested in the passing of London pigeons than the theatrics of his employer. Such a sensible boy.

"Mr. Silkin, while I consider your proposal — and forgive me but I'm sure you will understand the need for some careful thought on my part — I wonder whether it might not be beneficial to you to see what exactly it is that I am doing. After all, you are effectively proposing a business partnership and I would feel very uncomfortable were you not in full possession of the facts."

He thought for a moment but it was more theatre play, I had just offered him the opportunity to gather information about me and my practices, he was a fool certainly but not *that* stupid.

"Why not? I admit I'm curious about this stuff you're selling."

"And so you should be, it is an entirely new compound and you would hardly be doing your part as a purveyor of… chemical entertainments… were you not abreast of the latest developments. Who knows, perhaps between the two of us we can achieve more than would have been individually possible?"

That did it, I saw the piggy little light of greed in his eyes.

"Maybe."

I smiled, one of my best and most comforting smiles. One gets nowhere with people without developing something of a facial repertoire. "Marvellous. Then shall we take a stroll to the basement?"

2.

I run a small operation, I prefer it that way. I employ only those people I can trust and — a sad indictment of our age — they number but a few.

There is Goodwill of course — the man, not the notion; the name does not suit him in that sense — whom I have known for many years. In fact, in our school days we both took great pleasure in the exploration of arcane matters; an outmoded interest, even back then, but one which we pursued with great vigour. It was logical that when I became more… professional-minded to such occultism and the potential benefits therein, that he would be part of the venture. He takes care of the public side of things. I have never sought the company of my customers, happy to leave it to one who has no qualms about wallowing in the more dank areas of our species. He makes a good spokesman, erudite but blunt when needed, and with a face and physique that tends to solve any possible unpleasantness before it begins. Richard has a way about him that few would wish to disagree with, giving the — genuinely earned — impression that he would take to violence with zest and be sufficiently good at it as to be briefly instructive to whomever was testing him.

Then there is the ever baffling Yugo, my (al)chemist. A bizarre little man whom I picked up in Chechen. I can't say he's a great conversationalist, (or human being for that matter, he has the most bizarre turn of phrase and a disturbing odour to him, it has a hint of Brie and Thai Curry; I have no idea what he eats but it clearly provokes reactions in his biology which rivals his test-tube magic). Still, he has an amazing head for combining science and the occult and that is all I can ask.

I have some freelance assistance of course, menial slaves and enforcers but then they could hardly be considered staff, as the idiotic Silkin was about to discover as we entered the cellar, split as it was between Yugo's laboratory and the accommodation I chose to keep them in.

3.

"All very compact, I must say," Silkin burbled, attempting to hide his excitement behind a veneer of what he no doubt thought of as 'cool professionalism' but which came across as the burbling rhetoric of an estate agent.

"I see no point in wasting office space when I can so easily combine my work and comfort at home", I smiled. "It's a Regency house and has more than enough space for my rooms above and the business quarters below. I like my life under one attractive roof."

"Good for tax breaks too, eh?" he winked, ridiculous little snot that he was.

"Indeed... May I introduce Yugo, the scientific brains behind our operation."

Yugo had been, as usual, lost to the real world, head full of chemical reactions and compound formula no doubt, surrounded by the steaming glass containers of his workspace. He looked up once we entered the room and rubbed the steam from his thick glass lenses on the material of his lab-coat.

"Hello to meet you, I'm busy, go away now though", he mumbled, shaking Silkin's hand briefly before returning to work. I watched Silkin wrinkle his nose slightly and wipe the palm of his hand on his cheap-jack suit. He had noticed the smell, of course.

"We won't interrupt you long, my dear Yugo, as I am sure you are in the middle of yet more startling discoveries of great import."

"Found ancient formula for limb replication, cut off arm grow back like lizard, cool as cows if I could make work. Mongolian text hard reading though."

Silkin raised his eyebrows and looked at me, expecting confirmation that Yugo was as insensible as he seemed.

"You would be surprised at Yugo's successes, my dear Silkin," I said. "This is after all where 'Rebirth' was created."

"Yeah, I guess. Funny name by the way, sounds like hippy shit to me. The kids tend to go for more aggressive names these days; they like their drugs to sound sharp, y'know? Probably sell better if you did a bit of re-branding."

"Oh but the name is beautifully accurate. Besides, my market is a little more specific than you may realise, I think the name appeals to my... demographic... rather well."

Silkin put his hands in his pockets and started trying on the rôle of businessman once more. "That's the other thing, you're not going for the big client base. From what I hear you seem to be targeting quite small groups, I appreciate you need to keep your head down a bit in this game, but nonetheless it seems to me you stand to benefit from tying yourself in with me. I could get this shit on the streets into whole new areas."

"It's an interesting thought, but I'm afraid you still don't really appreciate what it is that I am selling."

"Drugs are drugs, mate; trust me on that. They make 'em high, make 'em slow, make 'em happy make 'em stupid... It's all about the next big thing." He fixed me with one of his attempted 'hard' stares again, saying "That's the only reason we're talking: you've got something new and that interests me, otherwise your boys would have been sent to bed with a few fractures and the conversation would have ended the minute I heard of you."

"You haven't tested it then?" I will admit that had been something that I had wondered on; not that he would have felt any effect had he done so, Rebirth has a very specific trigger and would have all the efficacy of Aspirin if taken by the wrong person.

"Fuck off, nobody gets successful in this game by being a user. I keep this straight." He tapped at his head. "That's what's made me who I am."

"Indeed it has." I will confess the urge to laugh at him was quite strong, but I needed only play this game a little longer. "As well, the biology of what makes us all 'who we are' is the key to what we're doing here. It is a rather closely guarded secret that not everybody you might meet on the streets shares the same physiological make up as you and I: there are... *creatures* out there who may look and act like us, but are different in one rather defining way."

Silkin was glazing over, I could tell; the conversation was heading into areas that he had no knowledge or comfort in. This scarcely mattered to me, as it was, after all, merely just a game.

"I first came into contact with them in India, travelling with my colleague Mr. Goodwill." I had noticed that Richard had joined us, stepping down into the cellar with a slight smile on his lips. He well knew my predilection for the theatrical and was good enough to indulge it. "Some of the more private households use them as a slave force, held in subservience one assumes by fear of exposure and the disgust of their peers."

"Look..." Silkin tried to interrupt but I held up my hand.

"Please, hear me out. Perhaps it would be beneficial to give you an illustration of my point." I gestured towards the passage that led from the laboratory in thick red brick (a wine cellar at one point in the building's history I'm certain, one can still catch the scent of faded grape). "Let us move through to the kennels, shall we?"

Silkin nodded, a brief glimpse of discomfort now visible, he was losing his show of authority already; how easy it is to break men who carry little in their chests but hot air. Aycliffe stood to one side, allowing Richard and

I to lead the way, while his employer made a show of barging along by my side, believing himself a man that never simply follows.

"You keep dogs?" he asked, no doubt reassured by the continuing sound of his self-important voice.

"Of a sort, Mr. Silkin, of a sort."

We stopped outside the first chamber: a large alcove which I had taken the precaution of sealing off with a sturdy door. I opened the small viewing window and gestured for Silkin to look.

I glanced over his shoulder at the faces inside, staring vacantly at the door, waiting for instruction to fill the pointless void that rested between their ears.

"These are aberrations, Mr. Silkin, mistakes. Humans who have taken the natural step of expiring only to reanimate after the fact. 'Living dead', 'Zombie', call them what you will." He sneered, sceptical, even as he looked through the window at the unmoving creatures inside. "I confess that this is not their natural state. The lurid pulp fiction of the bookshelf and cinema screen is quite wrong on that point, they could most certainly pass for normal were you to see one day-to-day. However, their body functions are retarded, limited, operating on some form of 'emergency power' if you will. Still able to walk, talk and function much like you and I but, under the skin, biology betrays their lie.

"I admit our knowledge of them is vague, nobody seems to quite understand how it is that they work, why they came back, how they continue to operate so successfully given that they are physically limited in a natural sense. Yugo and I have tried to solve the problem…" — such happy memories of days down here in the dark, up to the knuckle in the flesh and bone of enigma, working our way through the small quantity of specimens we had brought back from overseas — "…and believe me that this was most fascinating: they continue to be aware, Mr. Silkin, no matter what we did to them. Most illuminating. Not only had they experienced death and returned, but it seems they cannot experience it again whatever physical impetus one gives them to do so!" I sighed, a mystery has its charm, but nothing thrills me more than knowledge and I confess that the complexity of these reanimates and the way they eluded our investigation had me all the more determined to comprehend them inside out.

"One thing we did discover was a way of stripping them of that self-awareness that so clashes with our conventional view of such creatures, a way of stimulating what little of their physical system was left until the point of mental collapse. Once done, they truly can become slaves, as you see there: mindless automata waiting to be filled with whatever intelligence and direction we choose to give them. It takes time, of course; they appear quite dead once the drug has done its work but, with a little application and patience they can soon be up and about again serving a useful purpose."

"Listen mate…"

"I'm not your 'mate', Mr. Silkin, I would have thought that painfully obvious by this time, even to you coming here with threats, piss and wind, seeking to intimidate me into joining your employ. I am teaching you mysteries here, be good enough to try and understand them."

"I understand fine: you're off your fucking head." He nodded at Aycliffe who was, of course, good enough to ignore the gesture.

"What's that, Mr. Silkin? More threats pending? Perhaps some loud shouting and the waving of firearms?" He had been backing away throughout this little interchange and was already reaching inside his jacket for a gun of his own. "The sensible Mr. Aycliffe and I have already had a reasonable conversation and come to some agreements of our own. I am a sensible and appreciative man to do business with, and he is as courteous as he is ambitious. I'm sure you can imagine where the conversation took us."

Aycliffe shot his former employer in the shoulder before he had even retrieved his own weapon from its holster. It fell to the ground while its owner started the vulgar business of screaming. I held up my hand to Aycliffe to stop taking any further action and stood to one side so that Richard could move past me and take our guest in a firm grip. He placed a thumb next to the fresh wound and dropped the man to his knees.

"No more bullets gentlemen, they are loud and wasteful. I have something far more economical and exciting in mind."

Richard pulled Mr. Silkin — still wailing and shouting his profanities — a little further along the corridor to the gate that marked the kennel of my other more unconventional helpers.

"I do appreciate the necessity of intimidation, you see, Mr. Silkin. You have your guns and your 'Estuary shouting', and I have Mr. Goodwill here. In extreme cases, I also have a little something that I picked up from somewhere much further than India." I walked over to join them and pressed the switch that lifted the solid metal shutter in front of my hounds' cage. Mr. Silkin flinched, expecting to see some ravenous beast or another. He was visibly confused when the pen behind the shutter appeared to be completely empty.

"They are a curiosity, Mr. Silkin. Some say they are the origin of the Greek myth of Cerberus; although whether that is just the urge amongst scholars to knit ideologies together in a way that they can understand, I couldn't say. Certainly they seem to hail from somewhere…" I struggled for terminology, esoteric matters are always hard to discuss with the un-initiated, "…out *there*, beyond what we know of as the physical world. If there is a Hell, maybe they are guarding it, but as I have yet to note any real proof of the place; these things are always nebulous."

Silkin actually began laughing. "There's nothing there!" he shouted.

Which was when one of them began to growl… disturbed by the noise perhaps, or the innate sense of food nearby, tempting flesh just a thin fabric of reality away.

"Oh you can't *see* them, they are not for eyes like ours, but you can *sense* them," I dropped to my haunches, so as to talk to him face to face, "and, brought close to our world by abilities that you couldn't even begin to imagine, baited and teased, one might even begin to *hear* them as they prepare to make themselves felt on our plane." I smiled genuinely for the first time since this man had come into my house. "With only the smallest of encouragements…" I took hold of his arm, relishing it a little as the movement caused him enough pain to shout again, the hot air snuffles of my little guard dogs wet and tangible on my cheek, so close was I to the cage and, beyond the bars, the creatures themselves, adding "…one can even begin to *experience* them!"

I forced his clenching hand through the bars and suffered dreadful indecision. It was hard to know where to look: at the seemingly miraculous pulping and chewing of his hand as the jaws of my creatures set to their invisible consumption, or at the face of Silkin as he witnessed the same. I did my best to catch both.

I could even forgive his screaming now, yanked by the arm until he was taut against the bars, his face contorted against the metal, head squeezed hard, too big to pass through. His arm was unmade in mere moments; flesh, muscle and bone ripping, panting and splintering from the attentions of teeth unimaginable. I stepped back a little, cautiously kicking his splayed and twitching foot towards the cage in the hope that I could get it within reach of their claws. It fell short and I stood back, they seemed calm enough around me when at rest, knew their place and who was their master, but I didn't fancy challenging their selectiveness when in the grip of feeding. I imagine they would chew on anything placed within their reach.

There was a snap of dislocating bone as the arm was pulled free of its socket, then the most delicious surprise of a spraying welt appearing spontaneously across the crumpled cheek and eye which was squeezed close enough to the bars for them to reach. I watched the meat of his face pull away from the skull and hang at right angles — caught between clenched teeth I imagine — before it snapped free from the neck muscles and vanished with a wet pop, curling and slopping into the gullet of the hound.

Enough pleasure. "Chop the rest up and poke it through", I said to Richard. "We may as well have shot of all of him; it makes no sense to leave any evidence."

"All neat and tidy," he agreed.

I turned to Aycliffe, who I noticed with some alarm had been dreadfully sick in the corner. "My darling boy," I shouted, "how simply dreadful! If I had known you possessed such a delicate constitution, I would have warned you to look away."

I took him by the arm and noticed him flinch markedly; now here was a boy who would be doing what he was told for some time to come, as it should be. "Why don't we head back upstairs for a Brandy? I have a delicious Armagnac that I am *sure* will settle your poor tummy."

max

1.

Thackeray came to us with his discovery late the following afternoon.

I'd spent most of the day in the flat trying to convince my new-found cat to behave like a reasonable creature and cut down on the whole 'scratching my sofa' and 'biting on my fingers' thing. Thus far Mattie was having none of it; he was a cat who knew what he liked and took little notice of anyone trying to tell him otherwise.

I'd rung Danny to inform him of his cat's whereabouts, but he seemed only too glad to be rid of him. Cheeky bastard bit me on the ankle while I was on the phone, so I could see Danny's point.

Deciding I needed some fresh air and human company, I thought I'd swing by the club. Asking Mattie not to destroy the flat too much, I put some tuna fish in a bowl for him and flicked the telly on so he had company (it was some lousy cooking programme, but I felt he might pick up some tricks to perk his tuna up if he paid attention), and left him to it.

The club doesn't open until eight but there's always enough work to keep people out of trouble from about three or four onwards. Tom isn't a believer in early mornings and doesn't expect anyone else to be either, so you start to be able to rely on some sign of life around mid-afternoon, even if it's only he and Len drinking coffees and moving bits of paper accounting around as if they care what's written on them (of course Len *does* care, but knows his employer well enough to appreciate that *Tom* doesn't, so wastes little time these days in taking the paperwork seriously while he's in the room).

I'd picked up a vat of takeaway Cappuccino from the Italian Deli a few doors up, as the coffee machine in the club is just fine but it's a fag to bash and clean when only one person wants a cup, so we tend to rely on bringing our supplies in. It saves time and stress all round.

"Afternoon gentlemen", I said after Len had let me in. "And how are things in the world of entertainment?"

"Like pulling teeth as always," Len muttered. "Although the band went down well."

Debruvio and the boys, dear friends all… they'd been playing last night as well. I'd planned on catching it — or, more precisely, *her* — before Tom and I had got distracted with other business. I wondered if Tom had settled up with the horn section as he'd promised. Probably; he was good at that sort of thing.

We were sitting at one of the tables, avoiding anything more serious than the wiping of milk froth from our upper lips, when Thackeray started banging on the door. I say 'started' because he only stopped when Len opened it and saved the wood from his panicked knuckles.

"Thank God you're here", he sighed and — rather than joining us at the table — walked straight behindthe barand pulled himself a double scotch without another word.

"Do help yourself", Len muttered, ticking the mental stock take he always carried in his head.

Thackeray drained the drink and slammed the glass on the counter. "Sorry; dreadfully rude of me. I'll pay, of course."

"Don't be so ridiculous!" Tom said, "You'll get yourself another and then tell us what it's all about.

Len rolled his eyes but didn't really mind, it was unusual to see Thackeray in any other mood than one of old-school civility. He was garden party material, not a man who showed his emotions without editing them first.

Thackeray did as Tom had suggested and then pulled up a chair at the table. "It's James Pullman…" he sighed, taking a more gentle sip of his drink this time, "or — more precisely — what samples are left of him."

Tom leaned forward in his seat, knowing instantly that he wasn't going to like this. " 'What samples…'?"

"Well, I know it may seem insensitive as he was something of a friend of yours, but given the situation I thought it important to keep looking into this drug and its effects. So, I didn't just dispose of Joe's body; I performed an autopsy on it, took various samples, blood, kidney… and his brain." This last was the one he expected us to rebel at I could tell and, true, the notion of James'ames brain bobbing in a jar in Thackeray's lab brought a shiver of discomfort. Tom let him off the hook immediately though, desperate to get to the point.

"Understood; you needed to know what had managed to kill him."

Thackeray stared at us, deeply uncomfortable. "That's the point, I don't think the drug did. There wasn't even the vaguest spark of life in him when I found him; I'm more aware of the need to be sure on that than ever before. I've become very good at recognising the signs — the little clues to continued existence that are exhibited in the biology of reanimates — and there were none. But…"

"…What?" Tom was having to restrain himself a little I could tell.

"That changed. His brain shows signs of activity now. Tiny, barely more than a flicker, but…"

"…Life," I said, finishing his sentence.

Thackeray took more scotch and nodded.

"So," Tom said, "You're saying that you cut him open, reduced him to a few pieces of meat, and now it looks as though he was still alive after all?"

Thackeray looked at us and I swear I have never seen him so visibly upset.

"I was so sure."

Tom sighed, he was angry, obviously. He'd liked James, but at the same time, he knew Thackeray and his fastidiousness in his work. He was a very skilled doctor and a damned good man, I could see Tom weighing the situation up.

"It was a mistake and, if we're honest, there's not much that can be done about it, is there?"

Thackeray shook his head. "No. There's nothing of him to work with... he's just..."

Tom put his hand on Thackeray's arm. "Leave it. Let's concentrate on what this tells us."

"But that's the thing!" Thackeray cried. "I'm no more informed than I was before, bar the fact that we now know this stuff *doesn't* kill us! It damages us irreparably, of that I'm certain, but..."

"That alone is important and, being brutal, something of a relief", Tom said. "Have neither of you considered the fact that, if it became common knowledge that this drug could kill us, it would encourage people to take it? We already know how difficult some of us find this..." He tailed off, there was little point in him continuing.

"We could have had people desperate for the stuff, mass suicides", I said.

"Yes", Tom agreed. "People would have been drawn to it as a way out of their existence. Now all we have is a drug that fucks you up; nothing new there."

"But I still don't know how it works", Thackeray moaned. "It's not enough to analyse the little I have, I need to get my hands on someone else who has taken it. Most importantly, I need some of the drug itself."

Tom leaned back and reached for his coffee. "Well then, that gives us a plan doesn't it?"

"Erm", something had just occurred to me, "you said you needed someone else who had taken the drug?"

"Yes, knowing what I do now I could learn a lot more from them."

"Have we all forgotten Fat-Boy?" I said. "I don't know what your boys did with him, Tom, but presumably he's still alive as well."

There was a pause and Tom leapt from his seat and towards the phone, "I only hope they didn't dump the poor bastard in a furnace somewhere!"

2.

I'd never been to the London Wetlands Centre, not being a man who can get all that excited by the combination of marshland and ducks. Just not my sort of thing is it? Certainly not at night either: freezing my rocks off, listening to Chas and Dave argue over who had the biggest spade.

"Would it be in poor taste to leave them to it, while we popped into The Bull's Head for a pint?" Tom whispered.

"What and miss the opportunity of bumping into Bill Oddie?" I replied, flicking my cigarette end at a Moor Hen that had been giving me the evil eye. "No chance."

"Got 'im, Mister H." Chas called.

"Dear God!" Thackeray, looking around in some agitation, never had he been so out of his element. "Announce it to the whole area, why don't you?"

We moved closer as Chas and Dave slipped around in the mud, trying to pull the weight of the man who had started all this out of the hole they'd dumped him in and onto a patch of grass nearby.

Thackeray was on his haunches and trying to wipe the mud from the man's face with his handkerchief.

"Doesn't look very alive to me", said Dave, leaning over the man. Which is how he was in the perfect position to get a face full of the mud and marsh water that the man expelled from his mouth and lungs. We all jumped back in panic.

The body was still again and we slowly crept back around him, Dave wiping at his face with the sleeve of his overcoat. "Then again…"

Thackeray went back to examining him before looking up at us. "Difficult to tell, we'll have to get him to my place where I can clean him up and give a proper examination."

We all looked at one another for a moment before I sighed and grabbed at an ankle. "Cop a limb then, let's get it over with."

3.

It took us half an hour of losing our grip on the muddy dead weight and falling over from time-to-time, but eventually we made it back to the boys' van and loaded him in the back. By then, all of us were in severe need of soap and alcohol. Thackeray was quick to offer us the use of his hot water in the guest rooms — my God, but the man has money — and, as his place was close and his cellar well stocked, we all took him up on it.

Straight to the showers then, Tom, Chas, Dave and I drawing lots on who got to use the two guest bathrooms first. I cheated — toss a coin quickly near Dave and he'll believe anything you tell him, distracted by the bright shiny thing in front of his eyes — but felt no guilt as I stood under the hot jet and scrubbed myself with rather pungent lavender soap.

Once we were all a little more presentable, we settled in his lounge with a large glass of brandy and the warm glow of a log fire (some people just *know* how to live). It was clear from the off that Thackeray was a little uncomfortable with Chas and Dave being in the house; don't get me wrong he's a great guy, but so woefully old-fashioned you could see he was partly convinced that they would start chewing the furniture or maybe shit on the rugs at any moment. Then again, both Tom and I chuckled to watch the boys terrified to move, as it was clear that they were feeling as much of a clash of cultures as their host, terrified that one false move would see them breaking something they didn't even know the name of.

Thackeray was eager to get straight-on with his examination of the body — "Louis Del Grande", according to the cards in his wallet — but none of us really wanted to watch, even though we all knew it was unlikely to involve anything particularly gruesome. For myself it was the vacancy of the man that I found most disturbing, the absence of any real sign of intelligence or personality. Chas was the only one of our company that hadn't experienced death; that moment when you feel yourself slipping, closing down... then NOTHING. In our case, that would be followed by becoming aware again at some point after. Reanimates varied, some were up and about again at speed, while others — myself included — went through a period of confusion both mental and physical, the brain trying to reassert itself, trying to get back to the all important business of functioning, only to find muscle degradation or simple fear getting in the way. When I looked at Campbell, I was reminded of that time: that vanishing into absence only to come back filled with fear and paralysis. In his case, that paralysis seemed absolute, which was the fear of us all: the thought that we might end up there again one day, unable to move, a prisoner of flesh and a dumb brain but still *alive*. It was a fear that had no solutions, either that was our future or it wasn't; we would all find out one day.

When Thackeray joined us, it was with a sigh as he dropped into an armchair, then accepted a drink from Tom and sat there for a few moments without saying anything. Eventually, he poked at the fire, threw another couple of logs on it and confirmed what we'd been thinking.

"He's definitely alive, but severely compromised mentally. It's like a person with advanced Alzheimer's: physically ticking over, but barely able to rationalise or think for himself. As far as I can tell anyway", brushing his comments off, tired and lacking a degree of faith in his abilities after what had happened to James. "It's so difficult to tell when there's so little response. There's nothing to work with, I have only guesswork and the little data I can collate."

"You need the drug itself", Tom said, reminding him of his earlier comment.

Thackeray nodded. "Well, that's all that's left, isn't it really? And if I can't make head nor tail of that, then there's no hope of understanding it."

Tom thought and then moved to stand by the fire. "Well, I suppose we'd better go and get you some then." He said this lightly, before then flashing one of his gap-toothed smiles and finishing his drink in a toss.

4.

Tom vanished to make a phone call, while I began to feel that familiar unease build in my gut. Invariably when Tom mentioned 'we' doing something, it would be a short space of time before that settled to 'me' doing something, while Tom egged me on from the sidelines with a glass of Merlot and a stuck-up thumb.

Actually though, it turned out I was wrong on this occasion because Tom had the opposite in mind.

"Just spoken to Danny", he said once back in the room, "and found out where Waugh tends to peddle this stuff — goes by the name of 'Rebirth' by the way…"

"Hardly accurate", Thackeray muttered, sinking deeper into his chair.

"The sensible way of getting hold of a sample is to go and buy some. It would be a mistake to go mob-handed, we don't want to draw attention to ourselves. I don't really relish the idea, but I think I should do it, with Max keeping an eye out for me." He glanced at me with a smile. "If we're being realistic, I stand more chance of appearing old and sufficiently at my wits' end with existence than you do."

"I won't argue", I said, returning the smile.

"Good." He clapped his hands and made to shake us into action, adding "Tomorrow I shall revisit the lawless days of my youth!"

5.

Tom — most especially when he had had a glass of wine or two — would often talk about his youth on the stage. Indeed if only the critics and his peers had possessed half of the sense of wonder about his performances that he did, he may have been able to work at it longer than he did. Sadly, the only wonder many of them had offered was that someone had given him the part in the first place. Not to say he was dreadful — in fairness he wasn't — but he certainly had a habit of thinking that the play centred around him. There's only so many times you can walk on stage as 'Soldier 2' and hijack the production for the next five minutes with your ad-libbed speeches and constant upstaging before someone's going to replace you. He just didn't have the patience that I had had in the business: happy to play the bit parts for as long as it took, before someone noticed you and offered you something bigger. Mind you, that chance never came for me, so maybe he was right to grab his few moments when he could.

To look at him now though, you'd think he'd never left the stage. He was jumping at this chance for theatricality with gusto, no question. He had changed his usual blazer and jeans for a tatty suit, overcoat, woollen scarf, and worn leather gloves.

"I'm not sure you really have you finger on the pulse of the drug market", I suggested. " 'Ere, Granddad! Fancy some blow?!' "

"That's the point though, isn't it?" he replied. "This isn't a normal drug and clearly it isn't selling to the usual hoodie and baseball cap brigade. I'm creating the impression that I am a weary old man on his uppers!"

"Certainly on something... possibly Steradent... Still, if you're sure...?"

"Of course I'm not bloody sure! I'm not in the habit of buying drugs on street corners, am I?"

"No, sorry. Are you ready though?"

He sighed, "Yes, I suppose so." He drained the whisky he had been chugging — 'Dutch Courage', of course — and we headed out of the club and on to Soho streets.

I find London strange, a crowded mess of contradiction and noise. Tom loves it and knows the place with that fervency that you only seem to find in the most dedicated of London dwellers. He's told me time and again the little histories, the bizarre tales and anecdotes of the streets around the club, tales of De Quincey, Karl Marx, De Gaulle, of the notorious *Tableaux Vivants* at the Windmill Theatre and the nights of debauchery at The Coach and Horses. And it's interesting, it really is, but more and more I felt that my heart had become out of step with urban life. I had moved there from drama school — because for a trained actor to do anything else was commercial suicide — and stayed there now, like many of our kind, because there was a comfort in numbers. Danny Jerusalem was right when he talked of mankind's love of communities, of forming groups and gangs. Still, I was coming to realise how little it really fitted me. I can still get lost on the Underground for God's sake, even now after nearly twenty years. Ridiculous.

"Okay," Tom whispered, "make yourself scarce."

He walked ahead of me up Frith Street and towards Soho Square. I crossed over and suddenly felt ridiculously obvious, hands in my pockets and trying to look like I was just another man about his business, taking in the night air. It was a conscious effort not to start whistling.

Tom reached the edge of the grass and loitered, uncertain of himself for a moment. Then he walked around the little park and towards a bench. It was empty; they all were, except for a pair of Japanese tourists checking their map in the streetlights, frantic to find Tottenham Court Road and a tube back to their hotel. Normally you couldn't move around here for young 'emo' kids heading towards the Astoria, but they seemed to all be at home sorting out their hair dye, weeping gently to themselves, and writing bad poems probably.

Tom sat down on the bench and looked around, pulling his tatty coat around him, through nerves rather than cold. After a few minutes, I began to feel even more obvious wandering around the edges of the little park, so I stepped into a phone box on the corner. I was hoping that anyone watching would assume that I was calling whoever I had been waiting for as they hadn't turned up. I picked up the receiver and made a show of putting a few coins in and tapping at the buttons. The phone rang out in my ear, just as it should; it was my number and there had been nobody but me to answer that line for many years. Maybe Mattie would pick up, ask me to pick up more tuna...?

I noticed a man walking towards me, Asian guy, nice suit, empty face — nothing unusual about that, this was the world of corporate film and acting agencies, after all. I started talking, just in case, a bit of blather, he walked past the phone box and suddenly stopped. He turned and stared straight at me, his face utterly vacant.

"So, yeah, just wondering if you're heading down then…" I burbled, staring straight back at him but trying not to. Suddenly I realised I was looking at a reanimate too.

As I've mentioned before, there's just something about us; we flag one another pretty easily, the un-dead form of 'Gaydar'…

Maybe he was after the same thing as us, had me pegged as the seller. No, that didn't make sense; why wouldn't he assume that I was just another un-dead guy chatting to a… maybe that was it, like me he recognised a fellow reanimate but hoped I was dealing. Or maybe *he* was the dealer and was considering offering me some of the drug… the question was what to do about it. He continued to stare, took another couple of steps closer, now he was almost hemming me in. I began to feel very trapped in my silly little box and wondered how much scarier it might be were I to just talk to him.

I put the phone down and stepped out of the box. "Hello mate; just calling a friend, y'know?" My, but this was going well already. "Lost my mobile."

Which was exactly when the bastard thing decided to ring in my pocket.

I flinched violently and then began tugging at my coat to pull the phone out, while nonchalantly saying "Well now, would you believe it? It was in my pocket all along!" I got the phone in my hand and stared at for a second… 'том' it said on the screen, a moment of uncertainty, then I answered it. The man in the suit continued to stare, saying nothing.

"Where did you bugger off to?" Tom asked. "So much for watching my back; been and gone hasn't he? Lucky I didn't…"

"Tom," I interrupted, "I'm right behind you, other corner of the square…"

The man — who it would seem was not the dealer — continued to stare, face slack, arms by his side, staring…

"Well what are you doing there?" I heard from both the phone and from several feet behind me, as Tom began walking in my direction. I cut him off.

"Friend of mine"., I said to the man in the suit. "Better be going really, things to do…"

He suddenly moved, dipping his hand into the inside of his jacket. I gave a panicked little noise as he whipped it back out again, a small plastic bag between his fingers. "Rebirth?" he said in a monotone voice. "Make you feel?"

"Already got some thanks," said Tom who was now stood right behind me. "Come on Max."

"Rebirth?" the man asked again, holding out the bag. "Take some and remember. Feel the rush, the pumping of blood, the pounding of a heart, the swelling of lungs. Take some."

"Seriously, we're fine for now, thanks, bit of a lightweight me…" He grabbed my arm and I felt Tom move closer.

"Take some!" he suddenly screamed, his face contorted but somehow still empty, the mouth was wide but the eyes were dead, a man not in control of his own actions. I tried to pull my arm away but he had a good grip.

"Look pal," Tom said, stepping in-between us, "push off, will you? My friend's not interested and neither am I." Tom went to take hold of the man's free arm when it lashed out, catching Tom on the side of the head and knocking him over in surprise.

The man in the suit was losing it, grabbing my other arm now, the small packet of pills pressing against my elbow as he pushed against me. "Take some! Take some! Take some!"

I kicked at his shin, *hard*; there was no reaction so I went for the crueller blow and still — even though his knackers must have been ringing from the toe of my boot — he didn't move, didn't let go...

Tom was back on his feet and he went for the man from behind, kicking at the back of his legs, hoping to bring the bastard down by wrapping his arm round his neck. It was like climbing on a statue, he looked ridiculous.

"Take some! Take some! Take some!"

I wriggled and tried to twist out of his grip. Tom had let go of his neck now and swung a punch right at his face. Tom yelled as the impact cut his knuckles and I flinched as a tooth and some spittle hit my cheek.

"Take some! Take some! Take some!"

It had a slightly wrong sound now after the punch to his mouth, but still he was sticking to the hard sell. Using all his weight, Tom threw himself against the man and we all toppled over with me managing to get one arm free. I pulled myself to my feet immediately, but the man in the suit was slower. Now that the balance of weight had shifted things were looking up. I yanked at the one arm still in his grip and kicked the pit of the arm that still held me, pulling it free.

"Let's go!" I shouted, only too aware that the noise had brought the attention of passersby — what was it I said about London? I take it back, love the place, you can have a fight in the middle of the street and nobody steps in.

Tom and I legged it, the man in the suit still shouting as we ran.

"Take some! Take some! TAKE SOME!"

6.

Back at the club and both of us were feeling wired, disturbed, bruised and generally 'out of sorts'. Luckily, two forms of assistance lay waiting for us: Thackeray and the bar. Personally, I leaned more towards the latter as being the most likely source of aid. I'm a great believer in the power of medicine and the prescribed pharmaceutical. I also tend to believe that nine times out of ten that pharmaceutical should come with crushed ice and a slice of lemon, repeat dose until problem has been forgotten.

We went through to Tom's office thinking, rather sensibly, that the examination of drug packets should not be performed by the owner of a club in front of punters.

"Obviously I can't tell a thing without running tests on it, but hopefully we could be on the way to something a little more constructive." Thackeray was beginning to appear a little more like his old self; which was good, there are some people who should never seem uncertain, their certainty being a universal constant that tends to make all the people around them feel a little more content in the general 'rightness' of things. Thackeray, as a doctor and all round clever chap who 'knows his onions', was definitely one of those people.

"Did you have any luck talking about this with your friends in high places?" Tom asked while selecting a record to play, never one to talk in absolute silence if he could avoid it. "Ah… 'Swiss Suite'!"

"Not much, it's a tricky situation really. The official world cannot be seen to act directly in this, for everyone's sake. At the moment, the only thing Waugh has done is manufacture a drug that affects reanimates; he's not even making that big a business of it. We can't offer evidence of him *selling* that drug because none of us could testify without drawing undue attention to ourselves."

Tom tapped his foot in time to Oliver Nelson and his band and nodded. "Basically, unless we catch him out at something else, he hasn't committed any crime we could actually pin on him without dropping us in it."

"Precisely."

"Which leaves us no better off at all then", I added, just for those who needed a little more fatalism.

"We have this." Thackeray held up the drug. "And while I may not be able to get anything from it, there's always the chance that I can find some kind of… I don't know… antidote, immunity, or something."

"Which all rather relies on someone who has taken it wanting to change their mind immediately," Tom noted. "Unless you mean that you may be able to reverse the ultimate effect that we've seen in Campbell."

"Sadly not. I fear Mr. Del Grande will never be able to function at full mental capacity again, although it has become clear that a degree of 'retraining' is possible. He is capable of everything we are, just not the intelligent reasoning to act it out. Still, he responds to me when I talk to him and — slowly mark you — has begun responding to basic commands: 'sit down', 'stand up', that sort of thing. He still retains the capacity for speech too, just nothing to say. He started mimicking me while I was recording notes, quite disturbing at the time actually."

Tom and I glanced at one another, we were having the same thought.

"The dealers", I said, determined to get there first.

We told Thackeray about the strange man who had attacked me, with Tom adding the fact that the supplier he had actually bought the drug from had a rather vacant — if considerably less homicidal — way about him too.

"It's possible, I suppose," Thackeray admitted. "With a degree of training, teaching them speech and actions — both things they may even retain a sub-conscious understanding of — given Campbell's response in a mere twenty four hours or so, there is little doubt that over a matter of weeks, or even months, he could be trained to show a modicum of normal functionality, although it would be a sham — 'learned' rather than 'genuine' behaviour."

"Like talking parrots", I suggested, wishing I hadn't as they both looked at me a little funny. "Except, you know, more Asian... better dressed, more into selling drugs... forget I said it."

"I get your point", Thackeray smiled. "Parrots mimic the intonations of our voice without having the vaguest notion of what they're actually saying; however meaningful or clever they sound they're just making a noise. It's not a bad analogy."

"No, it wasn't was it?" I smiled and raised my glass at them, glad to be proven intelligent. "Now, if you'll excuse me gentlemen, I need to go and feed my cat!"

I was ruminating on how cool that was as a parting shot — and finding that actually it was a little warmer than I had hoped when my brain farted it into my mouth — as I cut back through the club and onto the street.

"Night, Mr. Jackson" Dave said, slightly on autopilot but the thought was there.

"Night, mate."

I cut across the road and begin my way towards the tube, an early night for once. Mind you, I would have to start thinking a little bit about that in future, what with my new-found responsibilities through cat ownership. I would hate to think that I was a bad parent... erm... owner. Oh bloody hell... I was on the slippery road to middle age, wasn't I? Just because of a damn cat. Next thing you know I'll be staying in to watch *Tom and Jerry* with the little bast—

"Take some."

Oh fuck...

As much as Auberon placed utter conviction in the effectiveness of his little meat puppets, I had decided it was more than prudent to keep an eye on them.

It was a neat idea, no question: they had neither the brain nor motivation to act against our best interests, could say nothing of importance if questioned, were utterly trustworthy when it came to handling the money or supply — after all, why would they have any interest in either, as they were no longer mentally built in those terms — and, of course, they worked for free.

In a line of work where staff were a constant issue — especially if one had hopes of expanding as we certainly did — the solution was stunning in its simplicity.

Still, I had concerns leaving them on their own — at least until we had completely assured ourselves of their reliability. It's attention to detail like that that makes me who I am. As brilliant as he is, Auberon has altogether too much confidence in his abilities and that breeds assumption. I don't like assumption, never have.

So, I keep an eye. I make sure things are running smoothly. I make sure all is well.

And tonight was beginning to prove how right I was to have done so.

I'd been grabbing a drink at The Toucan — slack perhaps, but I was two minutes away and thirsty — when the trouble had started.

"Some sort of fight kicking-off in the Square", I overheard someone say as I was stepping out to check-up on things. I arrived just in time to see one of the puppets, bedraggled and shouting, moving off down Frith Street in pursuit of, I assumed, a pair of clients. My first thought was that he had been mugged by someone desperate enough for the drug, but poor enough to fight rather than pay for it. We had little issue with that; as long as the freaks were taking Rebirth, it would do its job. Still, my inclination is towards covering all the options and I phoned Auberon as I followed them to let him know the situation.

If nothing else, we needed to tag the junkies and make sure we knew where they were. The last thing we needed is more collateral damage. Losses are inevitable in any business but we had misplaced altogether too many of them of late for my liking.

I kept my distance, the puppet had stopped screaming as he had lost sight of them around a corner and I held back, trusting its ability to place them soon enough. The things were like sniffer dogs; what they had lost in humanity, they seemed to make up for in more primitive animal instincts.

It shuffled along the street, seemingly content with its route and I followed on thirty feet or so behind, happy that I could just walk away if something indelicate occurred; there were a few people about on the street and I had no wish to be seen as in partnership with the thing. If it suddenly snapped and started attacking strangers, there was nothing on its person that could tie it to us and the best course of action would certainly be to cut my losses and melt away. Still, I would give it the chance to be useful for a little while longer.

It ended up just along the street from a small nightclub; 'Deadbeat', according to the sign outside. Jazz music filtered second-hand from the doorway and I watched it stare at the door for awhile, seemingly confused.

After a few minutes, it moved further along the street, found a doorway that offered it some shelter, and just stood there waiting.

Looking around, the street was quiet enough that I might be able to walk past the club and deal with the creature without drawing too much attention. It looked as if it had given up on trying to find the men it had been chasing, and was now little more than a loose end. I reached inside my jacket and removed the long-bladed knife I had taken to carrying there, sewn into a handmade sheath just beneath the armpit. A knife is a good weapon, effective, quick and — if one knows how to use it — subtle. That idiot Silkin and his love of guns would never grasp that, of course. To that sort, carrying a weapon was part of showing off; to a professional, it should simply be an occupational necessity, worn and used with an eye to practicality and effectiveness, rather than as some childish proof of masculinity.

I couldn't actually kill it, of course, but I knew from experience that if I caused enough brain damage it would be suitably immobile to appear so. It wasn't perfect, but if I could get it out of sight for long enough I should be able to do enough of a hack job on it to make it pass examination. 'Lesser of two evils': if it was going to be unreliable, I didn't like the idea of it wandering around here. There was a small alleyway between where it was hiding and the club, if I could drag it down there I would have privacy to work.

I slipped the blade up the arm of my jacket, cradling the hilt in loose fingers so that I could walk casually and not draw attention to myself. Then I started to make my way up the street. A couple of people stepped out of the doorway of the club and stood on the pavement laughing. This was not good... I didn't want an audience. I crossed over and reached for the mobile again. To kill time, more than anything else.

"Auberon?"

"My darling boy, what's the news? Solved our little problem yet?"

"Working on it, the puppet followed them as far as a nightclub, Deadbeat, jazz place."

"Oh, how delightful... what's the wine list like?"

"I wouldn't know, I'm waiting on the other side of the road a few feet away. It's hidden itself in a doorway at the top of the street, I'm just waiting for the right moment to dispose of it."

"In the middle of the street? You'll have your work cut out!"

"I know but in the absence of any other ideas…"

"If you can wait, I'll come in the car, that way you can bring it back here and we can get rid of it properly."

I sighed. He was right of course. I just hated the idea of the thing hanging around, ready to do something I might regret.

"Fine, I'll wait." I gave him the address and walked back down the other end of the street where I was more hidden from the door of the club.

I just hoped he wouldn't be too long.

Twenty minutes had passed when a man walked out of the club and the puppet twitched in its doorway, suddenly alert once more and watching him as he walked towards my end of the street. It stepped from its hiding place and started following at speed. This could only have been one of the men it was following earlier. Still, there was no sign of Auberon and the car.

Choices.

Decisions.

I watched as the man lit a cigarette and turned left out of the street, completely unaware that the puppet was right behind him, mere feet from his back. What to do…?

The street was empty; that perfect time of the night when everybody's found where they're going but nobody's ready to leave yet… give it an hour and the pavements would be full again as people went home or onto another late-licence drinking hole.

I ran quietly to catch up with them.

"Take some, take some, take some!" the puppet was saying, holding up a little bag of Rebirth as it did so…

The man looked 'round, startled, frightened too, and he was just in time to see the puppet bearing down on him and me right behind with my knife drawn.

"Take some!" it shouted. I ran the blade across its throat before it had chance to draw any more attention with its shouting.

"Jesus!" the man hissed, as I pulled the creature around, swinging my legs out at the same time so that this man he'd been following was swept from his feet. I didn't want either of them running.

The puppet was going wild, still trying to shout but no throat left to do it with. The blood was minimal of course; it always is in reanimates, their circulation is too slow, you just don't get the same spray as you do in a living target. I brought the knife down hard in its left eye and, using the flat of my palm, made the blade swivel in the socket causing as much damage to the brain behind as I could in one blow. I grabbed the handle as the puppet dropped, motor function shot, and used its body weight and an upward swing of my arm to wrench the blade free. Now the witness.

I had to assume he was a reanimate also. Unlike Auberon, who seems to be able to place them at a glance, I've never been quite as good at spotting the signs. He was getting back to his feet and managed to raise his arm to block the first knife strike which had been heading for his throat — not that he was shouting right now, they never actually do in that situation. Whatever you see in the movies, they're always so occupied with trying to stay alive that speaking or calling for help never occurs to them. I kicked low at his leg which was pushing him back to his feet so that he fell again, making a grab for his hair at the same time, the result being his head and throat opened up for the knife and it was the matter of seconds to shove it straight into...

max

My face contorted as I fell backwards. There was a brief glimpse of the knife blade shining in the beams of a distant streetlight, and then he twisted around due to Dave's firm grip on his wrist and the knee in the base of his spine.

The guy was good though, using the momentum to his advantage by turning the knife in his attacker's direction. What Dave lacks in intelligence — which is a lot — he more than makes up for in weight, strength and knowing how to put another man down. He altered the grip he had on the man's wrist and, instead of trying to fight the new swing, he increased it by pulling the blade down and back towards the man holding it. The knife went into his gut, and he had the good grace to look surprised and then pissed off. Dave yanked upwards, finishing the job in a manner that felt a relief at the time, but would chill me later; the almost thoughtless way in which the bouncer took another man's life, even one who had been trying to do no less to me.

"You alright, Mr. Jackson?" I nodded, then — noticing the state of my sleeve and the smearing of blood from the cuts the knife had made — wondered if I had been lying. The sound of a car coming had me on my feet and moving, autopilot kicking in; this would not look good.

"Richard?" a voice asked as Dave looked over my shoulder at the car, then he let go of the man and stepped back, as uncertain as I how this was likely to play out.

The killer ("Richard", I assume) stumbled into the road, stopping in the lights of the car like an actor hitting his spotlight, reached out a hand (to what I couldn't tell, it seemed a random response but then all manner of things are likely to go through your head at the moment of death, trust me *I know*) and then he dropped face first onto the tarmac.

There was a pause as this sunk in and then the car sped over to us and we ran. Not the most sensible of reactions perhaps, but it wasn't something we were thinking about. I glanced over my shoulder to see the man who had shouted pulling the dead body onto his back seat which told me that he was as unlikely to be discussing this with the police as we were.

He was reaching for the freaky pusher by the time we turned the corner towards the club.

waugh

1.

My first experience of Richard Goodwill was the feeling of his fourteen-year-old fist pounding into my jaw. It was a good punch, strong and well placed, and the sound of the playground chanting — a chorus of encouragement no less bloodthirsty or enthusiastic as one imagines the crowd at a Roman circus to have been — combined with the understandable sense of dislocation his blow caused, formed an almost transcendental buzz in my mind. I was no stranger to such victimisation, my early school life was filled with such random flurries of violence and disgust; I didn't take to my peers nor they to me. It didn't bother me overly, even then I rolled with the blows and remained confident of my superiority mentally if not physically, the victor of such disputes is not always the one with the strongest arm after all, one can lie bleeding and bruised yet superior in principle. Besides, physical pain has never been something to displease me... there is a certain liberation to the opening of wounds, the snapping of bones; one can understand and savour quite delicious moments in the throes of such physical endurance.

Lying on the dirty grit of the playground, surrounded by the arcane chalk marks and graffiti of the young, I looked up at my attacker and saw him for what he was: an almost godlike statue of youth, good looking and adored by the crowds but also a politician, he knew what he was doing even then; acting to the crowd and asserting dominance and control amongst those that saw him. I understood his actions and, even with the taste of blood from a cut cheek in my mouth and a stabbing pain in my head, I fell in love with him a little. He was a powerful and beautiful boy.

2.

I don't have a great capacity for physical exertion, my body is thin and my muscles underdeveloped. Still, like all of us, I am only too capable of acting against my natural preferences when forced to do so. Having pulled Richard's body into the car I gritted my teeth and lifted the troublesome puppet on top of him, feeling something pop in my back as I did so; a little pain, no serious concern. I closed the door on the two of them, uncomfortable at the thought of Richard having to endure such indignity, though assuredly he was beyond such considerations. All in all, it was the work of seconds and the only two people to have seen that work take place were now my primary concern. Not that I was motivated by the need to cover up my actions, you understand. After all, they would not be telling tales — it was their crude attack that had necessitated it — but more because I had no intention of allowing them to simply walk away from it.

Revenge is such a petty little word — and certainly my urge to make them accountable could be marked as a practical one for reasons of both business and self-preservation — but, no, I am happy to admit my emotional faults. I have very little capacity for tolerance or forgiveness and a huge propensity for making people regret actions that displease me. By all means think me weak, I care little, I am a man with all the heart and stomach that goes hand in hand with that condition.

I pulled the car into the street which they had run along (although I was in little doubt as to their destination, as Richard had told me enough on the 'phone to make an informed guess) and drove quietly along until I found somewhere to park and think.

3.

Richard and I continued the next year or so as diametrically opposed players on the tawdry stage of state education. I was lost to my books and the almost pathological desire for learning which not only defines me, but had also marked me out for the brunt of his physical prowess as well as that of many others like him.

I watched him, of course — though I knew my attentions would most certainly never be reciprocated, even as a child I have never been prone to naïve fancy — both on the playing field and as he moved like a hero through the corridors and yards of the school, soaking up the respect and adulation given him by all; the boys who so wanted to be him, the girls who so wanted to own him... Richard was a ruler of men even in those days.

The change in him was something I noticed, so aware was I then of his bearing and attitude. I'm sure many people were blind to it; he made a good show, but it was as we entered our fifth term that I noticed there was something different in him, something dark and bitter. I ached to ask him of course, to find out what it was that was troubling him but as I say, I was no fool and knew that he was hardly likely to open his heart to me.

I was understandably surprised therefore when *he* approached *me*. I had been sat at the edge of the school football field, head in a book, idly tearing at grass with my fingers, enjoying that green smell, that feeling of perfect solitude one can get from being in the middle of an open space and quite alone.

"You're quite a reader aren't you?" His voice came from behind me and was startling, my first suspicion being that I was about to experience a repeat performance of my beating; I'll admit the notion did not displease me. However, he sat down a couple of feet away and looked out across the field. "I reckon you're a person who's likely to know a lot, especially given the sort of thing you're always staring at," he nodded towards my book, "when it comes to the occult and all that."

He was brushing the subject off, feeling self conscious about it, nothing new there, an interest (and belief) in such things was a brave step to take. It was so much more comfortable to take this world as a practical and immovable sphere, dismissing the possibility of deeper realities.

"I read a lot, yes." I wasn't sure what his interest would be, even then it could so easily have been a build up to a beating, using my interests as the habitual tool for mockery.

"Okay." He continued to stare, picking the heads off daisies and throwing them into the wind. "Tell me then, do you believe in ghosts?"

I thought for a while, the turn of conversation being unexpected. "Yes, I suppose so. There is definitely an existence beyond the flesh. Something more to all of us than meat. Why?"

"I want to know how to hurt someone."

"I wouldn't have thought you'd need my help with that."

He looked at me and smiled, rather gently. "Not usually but this one's different." He looked away again, returning to daisy throwing, adding "this one's dead."

4.

I have already confessed my love of the theatrical and I won't deny that my mind was turning to the Grand Guignol as I sat in the car and made plans.

Reaching over my shoulder I was, with some degree of discomfort, able to reach the knife still wedged in Richard's gut.

I called Yugo. Explained what I wanted him to do. Once he had stopped panicking, I explained it again and made it suitably clear that I was not open to a debate about it.

Richard would never have argued.

I reached over to the passenger side and opened the sun visor. Using the tip of a pen, I prised the mirror from its leatherette housing and carefully scraped the blood from the knife blade on the surface. One of the men had clearly been injured, while he ran he had cradled his arm. Hopefully the knife still carried a trace of him as well as the other two that its blade had tasted.

5.

Richard's problem was certainly a fascinating one. It concerned his father, a man whom — as is always the way — had made him the boy he had become. Never afraid to unleash the sharp sting of his leather belt, the back of his hand or (on one particularly drunken occasion) the sulphurous burn of a match on the sole of his feet.

Interestingly though, it wasn't the violence that had earned him so much loathing from his son; rather, it was the air of failure which the man had carried around his shoulders. He had been, to use the modern vernacular a 'waste of space', stuck in a dead-end cycle of low paid jobs that just about saw him through the doors of a bookmaker or off-licence. He had filled Richard's home with an overwhelming air of dismal apathy, of wallowing in acceptance of a life barely worth enduring. Rather than drag Richard down, it had increased his determination to be a success in a world that he knew his father had barely tasted. That conviction had, in turn, made his father all the more determined to drag him back down. And that was something Richard could never forgive him for…

He had come to the decision that both he and his mother — a taciturn creature who rarely made a mark on him as far as I can tell, someone who took to her victim-hood with resignation — were to be rid of the troublesome man and had pocketed a kitchen knife for the purpose. He had stood resolute, waiting patiently in the shadows of their front hall for the sound of a fumbled key in the lock of the door, eager to have the job done.

It was at two o'clock in the morning that his mother had been woken by the phone and the commiserations of the police that her husband had been run over on his way home from a night's drinking. Her son, still awake and still waiting for the opportunity to rid himself of the man he loathed, had been cheated of his victorious moment of liberation.

And Richard didn't like to fail in anything he set out to do.

If he couldn't kill the man, then was there still some way he could act out his desired revenge? To let the man who had been his father know that he had brought the violence of his son down on his head?

I began my researches.

There were certainly precedents; documents claiming to detail the raising of spirits for the purposes of communication were common. However, I struggled to find any guide to the punishment of souls by the living. Also, despite my interest, I was by no means sure that such perpetual existence as the human soul existed. It was a possibility of course and I kept an open mind, but I was by no means a blind follower of such religious doctrines. I was convinced of the efficacy of certain rituals of magick and occult principles, but a goodly part of me viewed such manipulation of people and reality as nothing more than an outmoded form of science. In fact, everything I've learned since has held me to that view. I don't consider the acts I perform or the products I sell to be anything 'magical' or 'fantastical', just scientific principles based on more ancient — and sometimes disturbing — principles.

But I did so desperately want to help him.

Which is why I did what I did.

6.

With the blood on the mirror, I dropped the knife into the glove box out of harm's way, and proceeded to wipe the congealing liquid across the surface with my finger, muttering the incantation under my breath. Words are to magick what numbers are to science: they are the building blocks of the reality we map and alter. A physicist reworks the physical world with his equations, I do it with syllables and rhythm.

I needed a match.

Patting my pockets I swore as I came up short, then remembered the lighter in the dashboard; 'hardly ideal, but hot enough' I imagined, popping it into its housing and waiting for it to heat up.

7.

The old man screamed, spittle flecking his booze-stained beard. Nicotine stained fingers spasmed in the air as he fought to pull his wrists clear of the wire I had bound him with. I wasn't worried though; he was weak with years of exposure and abuse; a life lived in doorways and underpasses doesn't make for strong men. Still, the noise can be a problem.

"And that's my father?" Richard asked, watching as I shoved the woollen hat the tramp had been wearing into his wide-open mouth.

"It is now, reborn inside this body."

"Amazing."

He walked over and seeing his face lit so dramatically by the flames of the small bonfire we had lit — which wouldn't draw too much attention, the forest around this small clearing was dense enough to keep the light from any of the houses that lined the area — I knew I had been right to help him. His eyes were filled with such beautiful certainty, such conviction and enthusiasm for what lay ahead.

He took the knife out of his coat pocket, the one he had planned to use on his father on that long and — ultimately pointless — night.

He looked to me for a moment, the first sense of unease creeping into him. I put my hand on his, let my fingers touch the metal blade of the knife.

"Go on," I said, "it's alright…"

He smiled and, after a moment began to carve.

I never told Richard that I'd lied about the ritual: that it was just some tramp I had noticed living in the woods by the school and that the incantation was powerless random words from *The Iliad*. But, even then, he was an intelligent man; I have no doubt he probably knew.

8.

I walked into the club and looked slowly around, trying to spot the injured man. The bouncer on the door stared at me, but I smiled happily and he seemed convinced of my simple intentions for fun.

I walked around, checking every table, then popped into the toilets, looking for the killer and his friend there. Nothing.

The band hit a crescendo and set down their instruments for a break, there was the swell of applause and people began to rise from their tables, no doubt heading for the bar. I got there first.

"Hello there," I said to the girl serving, all happiness and smiles, "a gin and tonic if you would be so kind." As she moved around preparing my drink, I added "Lime rather than lemon if you have it." She smiled and nodded, eventually placing the chilled tumbler down on the bar. I handed her a five pound note. "Another small favour if you could, a man came running in here with an injured arm a moment ago." She made to speak but I held up my hand to stop her. "Please, I don't wish a debate about it. I notice he's not here and so either he's already left, which I doubt, or he never came *in* which…" I thought for a second, "just doesn't seem likely. To follow a man twice to this location is just too much of a coincidence. He's here. And if I can't see him, he must be out the back somewhere. In which case you can get a message to him. I will be sitting just over there", I gestured to a table that was far enough away from the stage to be private, but public enough to stop anybody doing anything ridiculous, "and I will expect to talk to him and his big friend in five minutes or less. This will be his only chance for a meeting. If he doesn't come out, or someone very foolishly tries to evict me from the premises, he will find me in a less polite mood next time. He won't know when that will be, but you can assure him that should he be surrounded by as many of his friends as possible., I will be as ruthless dealing with them as I will him."

I took up my drink and went to sit down, watching the girl speak to a large man with a bushy moustache who glanced in my direction. I raised my glass and smiled. He vanished out of a staff door and I waited for company.

I sipped my drink; it was rather good.

max

1.

Tonight was going downhill rapidly. I have had many bad nights in my time of course; you don't live the sort of life I do without clocking-up some lamentable chunks of experience. Still, as regrettable as was the evening that I went home with a gorgeous lap dancer that would later reveal themselves to be a one-time plumber from Kent — "Ted" when off duty, he casually informed me as I stood withering in my boxer shorts — I think I can safely say that tonight was pipping it to the post as 'that night I should have stayed at home and watched the telly for a bit'.

Tom had already gone into overdrive the minute I had reappeared in his office with Dave in tow. Thackeray was still there, thankfully, and he grabbed the club's First Aid box and set to binding my arm, while Tom paced and tried to get some sense of calm perspective on it all.

"At least we don't have to concern ourselves with disposing of the body", he said, relieved perhaps that there was one silver lining to the particularly stormy cloud I had dragged into his club.

"It means that Waugh may be on to you though", Thackeray replied, pessimistic bastard.

"Yeah", said Dave, desperate to be part of the conversation.

"We ran like the clappers", I said. "With a bit of luck, he was far too busy dealing with the bodies to notice where we went."

"Let's hope that's the case", Tom agreed. "Mind you, even if he did trace you to here, I think we can safely say that it's unlikely he's going to be making a scene in the middle of a public club."

Which would be when Rachel came in from the bar and passed Waugh's message on. He was right outside, waiting for us — well, *me* — a thought that made all manner of conflicting opinions rush through my head, ultimately they all boiled down to one:

"We're fucked", I said and rubbed at my sore and bandaged arm so that I could remember what it was like to feel such a tolerable amount of pain.

Tom thought for a moment, then slammed his palms on the desk making Oliver Nelson skip a groove through the vibration. "If he wants a full-on offensive, he can damn well have one!" he shouted as he reached for the phone. "We'll go and have a chat with him with pleasure. First of all though…"

2.

He wasn't quite as I had imagined him. The Wildean trappings were there, the old fashioned suit and waistcoat, the oiled hair and pale skin; still he was younger than I had expected, maybe late thirties early forties, and his cheeks betrayed the pock-marked scars of a spotty youth even though he appeared to be wearing foundation to try and cover it.

Tom pulled Len to one side and explained what was going on, ordering a couple of drinks while he was at it. The last thing he wanted to appear was nervous; just a bunch of businessmen sitting down to discuss matters, all polite, all controlled...

Thackeray joined us — though whether through a desire to show a 'united front' or medical curiosity I couldn't say — but Dave went back to his position by the door. We were all agreed that his presence was neither constructive or necessary, whatever Waugh's wishes.

"So nice of you to join me", he said as we sat down, Rachel placing our drinks in front of us then making a hasty exit back to the relative safety of the bar.

"You asked so sweetly," Tom smiled, "we could hardly refuse."

"You're dead", Waugh said, sipping at his Gin and Tonic.

"Is that a threat or an observation?" I asked.

"Oh, an observation. I've yet to move on to the threat part of this conversation. I'm interested to know who you all are first. I presume this is your establishment?" he asked Tom.

"Yes", Tom replied, content to leave it at that.

"And you're the man at least partly responsible for the death of my friend," he pointed at me, "which makes you..." he looked to Thackeray, "what? His lawyer?"

"Doctor", Thackeray answered.

Waugh laughed. "Well now, there's a man planning ahead: he even has his physician on hand, should matters turn unpleasant. How forward thinking of you", his attention back on me now.

"It pays to be careful, you never know."

"Indeed not. Matters tonight do seem to be getting rather carried away, don't they?"

"Through no fault of mine."

Waugh's false smile vanished for a moment, to be replaced with something altogether more bloodthirsty. "Come now, because of you a good friend of mine is growing ever colder on the back seat of my car."

I held up my arm, "Self defence."

"True, but relevant only if I were being reasonable, and frankly", he grabbed my wrist — nearly knocking my drink over — and making me draw in breath, as his thumb caught the edge of the knife wound, "I'm not feeling particularly reasonable this evening."

Tom made to grab at Waugh, but he let go of me and held his hands up. "No. No fisticuffs; not here."

"What do you want, then?" Thackeray asked.

Waugh took a sip of his drink and leaned back in his seat. "To see who I'm dealing with. To get to know you. To… *understand*."

"That goes both ways", Tom said, as I rubbed at my throbbing arm and took a sip of my drink, trying not to look as freaked as I actually was.

"Ask what you like," Waugh smiled, "I don't mind discussing my business with you."

Thackeray folded his hands together, trying to look calm, I noticed his knuckles were white; he was no less angry than the rest of us, just trying to control it. "Why?"

"Why am I happy to discuss it? Because I have no intention of you presenting a problem to me, that's why. I'm proud of my achievements and happy to talk about them in such… *temporary* company."

"Ah… 'the threat part of this conversation', unless I'm mistaken", Tom noted.

"I meant 'why are you doing it?' ", Thackeray said, ignoring Tom.

Waugh shrugged. "Not 'how?' Your lack of scientific curiosity surprises me."

"The 'how' of it merely intrigues me, the 'why' *sickens* me; hence, I ask."

Waugh shrugged. "Basic business sense really: I have big plans which require a certain size of workforce. I have no desire to employ those whom I cannot trust, nor do I need to when I discover that I have such a readily adaptable populace on my very doorstep. I build a client list, I keep track of them — oh…", he looked at Thackeray, "a doctor… the piano player: you beat me to it on that one", referring to James Pullman of course. "As most of my customers take the drug at home, I make it my business to know where that is so that I can come and collect once they've over-dosed. Occasionally accidents happen — they take it in public, or someone like you finds them before I do — but nine times out of ten we just pop in and pick them up. You do live rather isolated and parochial lives…"

There was a pause as it sunk in.

"That's it?", Tom asked. "It's just about cheap labour?"

" 'Cheap'? Ha! *Very*; in fact, they pay me."

"You're destroying people — putting a drug in them that wipes their very self the moment it passes their lips — just to create a workforce?"

"Oh the drug isn't immediate. I tried that, but it was too much for the system, even one as hardy as yours. So, it requires a few doses before they are completely susceptible. But, otherwise, yes. You needn't seem so shocked, there are a number of historical precedents for empires built on the backs of slavery. Besides, it's little more than a farmer being criticised for utilising cattle, a hunter berated for training a pack of dogs…"

"We're talking about PEOPLE!", I hissed, trying not to jump to my feet and throttle him. Not that I was by any means sure that I could. Maybe it was the shock, but I was feeling decidedly light headed…

"No, I'm talking about freaks of nature." He smiled and leaned forward. "You're the new racial minority gentlemen. May I suggest you get used to the fact? As far as most of the world is concerned, you don't even exist. You have no rights, no recourse for help, no social worth… and if I have a use for a sorry bunch of…" he paused to think of the right term, then adding smugly, "*grave-niggers*", then all to the good. There's little you can do about it. After all, a number of you have come running to me already, desperate for that brief illusion of life. A few militants like yourselves are hardly likely to stem the flow of eager meat."

"Don't be so sure", Tom said. "I think you'll find us a little more capable than you give us credit for."

"Really? A nightclub owner who daren't make a scene for fear of exposure; a doctor who has a similar dilemma; and an idiot who's on borrowed time, if he would only just realise it? Hardly a major threat, now are you?"

"Borrowed time?" I really was beginning to feel rather rough… my stomach churning, my head pounding, sweat pouring off my… oh…

"I put it in your drink." I remembered the grab he'd made for me, his arm flashing across the table, my drink rocking as he clipped it with his hand…

"Oh, you bastard." I gripped my knees, suddenly aware of a sensation in my chest that I hadn't felt for so long: my heart *really* pounding… *ba boom ba boom ba boom*…

Thackeray came to my side, gripping me by the shoulders, reaching for a pulse, uncertain what to do.

Waugh brought his phone out of his pocket, Tom reached for his wrist instinctively, but Waugh laughed.

"Too late for that, old chap. As much as I may loathe these things, they can be dreadfully useful; text messaging particularly… now get your hand off me, you haven't the time."

He stared at me. "Listen to me…" I was trying, but it was getting hard to focus. "There are *things* out there", he gestured vaguely with his hand, "that you haven't the barest conception of. Reality is multi-layered and in-between those layers are creatures. Dreadful, insatiable things that patrol mindlessly, sniffing, hunting, preying on those foolish enough to try and pass from one level to another…"

"What are you talking about?" Thackeray spat, his rationalist mind rebelling at the sudden twist in the conversation. He looked to Tom. "We need to get Max out of here."

"You need to listen!" Waugh shouted, a few of the closer tables glancing our way. "The drug is the least of his problems. It's his first dose, so he's going to be struggling for a while, half an hour maybe; but that's not what will kill him."

God, but I was struggling to breathe. However much air I took in, it didn't seem enough… Waugh was bringing something out of his pocket, it looked like a small mirror, stained with something…

"These creatures can be caught and pulled halfway into this world, if you have skill enough." He grinned, full of himself. "Which I do." He finished his drink, got to his feet. "They're hard to control — virtually impossible, really — but if you can keep them just outside this reality, just on the *fringes*, you can hold them and — if you give them what they want: *flesh* — you can *use* them."

Tom stood up too, putting himself between Waugh and the door. He hadn't noticed that a large crowd of people had been slowly making their way towards our table; neither had I for that matter, I was far too busy trying not to start smacking my face against the table to stop the horrible rushing feeling that was building in my body.

"I'm not a big believer in this 'magic' nonsense, I'm afraid", he said. "It will take a little more than some Lovecraftian waffle to get the wind up me."

" 'Magick'? Just a science with which we explore the aspects of nature we have yet to comprehend. When I talk of my little hounds, it's not as an esoteric notion: you can take it from me that I am describing nothing less than a natural phenomenon which, right now, is on its way, chasing the scent of your friend here." He gestured towards the mirror on the table, although the point was lost on us. "He has two choices: stay here and watch the dogs tear everybody in this building apart, or run. If he runs, he won't escape them; he won't lose them, his blood is in their nostrils now. But... if he cares the slightest for any of you, he might just let you live." Waugh laughed, "Well, 'live' is a somewhat generous term isn't it? *Exist.*"

Tom grabbed him. "If such things really are coming, then it would be a great shame were you to leave before they arrived."

"Turn around, use your head, and then get your damn hands off me." Waugh was still jolly, the intensity of his threat re-enforced by his confidence. There were maybe thirty of them; reanimates rewritten to Waugh's design. Vacant and still, dotted throughout the club, forming a clear passage between our table and the door.

"The cavalry?", Tom sighed, letting go of Waugh.

"If you like. Feel free to try and start a fight, if you wish. I'm sure your security staff must have itchy fists by now. Be warned, though, that the first thing they will do at the sign of any further threat to me or my safety is not attack you, they will lash out at the closest customer and do their best to tear their throats out. Not ideal for business, I would think." He looked at me, "Still, if you stand there long enough they'll be caught in the slaughter anyway." He stared right into me. "Are you *really* that selfish?"

No. Of course I wasn't.

Fuck.

I began to run.

tom

1.

Life is often like Miles Davis: a chaos of noise fighting against one another to achieve the perfect whole. The ears take time to become accustomed. Does one listen to the trumpet? To the rhythm section? To the piano?

Tonight is a case in point.

Max. In danger and on the run. My instinct is to follow him; to help, if I can.

But then, there's the gang of gatecrashers ready to put a halt to as many innocent — or at least fairly innocent, I hate to have a bar filled with saints — people as they can.

Finally Waugh, the man that caused this melody, the trumpet if you will, walking away with a smile on his lips and a cocky swagger in ¾ as he makes to leave.

Trumpet, rhythm or piano…?

The trained jazz listener knows the answer of course: you listen to all three and get with the vibe.

2.

"My friends will loiter awhile, enjoying the ambience for a few minutes, so as to allow me sufficient time to be far away." Waugh placed his few belongings back in his jacket pocket and began to stroll towards the door.

"I had a feeling that might be the case," I said, listening to the jazz in my head. "Safe journey…"

Waugh smiled at my sarcasm and walked out.

End of trumpet solo.

I grabbed Dave, who was making to stop him, and pulled him close. "No, leave it; get after Max," I handed him my car keys saying, 'He's in trouble…*again*. Do what you can. Be careful.'

"'Kay, Mr. 'arris." I could tell he wasn't happy about it — he would be less so, if he'd been privy to the conversation at the table, and maybe I was a bastard for not filling him in — but Max had a head start and I wanted to make sure Dave could track him down… time was an issue.

End of piano.

Now… the rhythm section…

I reached for my phone.

danny

The phone rings in my pocket, a few bars of the *Bewitched* theme tune, what can I say? I'm a twat sometimes...

"Yeah?" An ear full of Tom Harris. "I'm on my way for God's sake! I'm being as quick as I can." He talks some more anyway, and I smile as Joe the Taxi — yes, after the song, what do you think? — puts his foot down and roars through a red light... he's a good mate... client... well, that's as close as I get to mates really...

Harris is talking about monsters... I don't really do monsters, but then I can tell neither does he.

"Glad to hear you two followed my advice and decided to keep your heads down then", I sighed. "Not much I can do right now, but I'll keep thinking and you can tell me more when I see you." I hung up.

"Fun night?" Joe asks.

"Yeah... shaping up to be."

max

And I'm running. With no clue or inclination as to what might be on my tail. In fact, no clear thought in mind whatsoever. An absolute mental cluster-fuck of random shouting, and the ever-present conviction that my heart is going to explode any second.

I can't imagine people doing this for fun, but then people get up to all sorts of crazy things in the name of recreation I suppose. There are those who have their genitals pierced and consider it an act of sensible and practical scarification, so what's a little adrenaline rush when you're looking for a pastime?

Shit, but it feels bad...

This was nothing like 'life' either. I remember 'life': it was smooth and beneath notice (except when ill health made you aware of physicality, of the difficulty of breathing or the aching of limbs). In fact, I'd say that one of the best things about life is that when you really have it you don't notice it. *That* is its real pleasure. Everything in its right place, the engine running clean...

My engine was sputtering, working on crude petrol, and oiled with shit...

Where would they come from? That was the issue. It was all very well running as fast as I could, but I could be aiming in their direction for all I knew. How do you outrun something that you can't see? Maybe don't even believe in?

No... scratch that... I believed in them. Waugh had been convincing enough on that point, I didn't take him for a man given to empty threats.

So where to go?

And how long did I have?

The only thing I could approach as a plan, was the need to gain ground as much as possible. It was a risk — for others more than me, I suppose — but I needed to move faster than my feet would carry me.

Poland Street, on to Great Marlborough, then Argyll... Oxford Circus and The Tube.

People were staring at me, my condition clearly obvious at a glance. Christ, but I could hardly breathe... the drug was getting more and more potent if anything... What had Waugh said? 'Half an hour'? It had been in my system now for maybe ten minutes and I was already struggling to move, let alone run... The tube was my only chance, put a bit of space between me and the creatures, wherever they may be.

I struggled to shove my Oyster card at the ticket barrier, vision blurring, all the time glancing over my shoulder for any sign of pursuit (I would later discover that Dave had been just behind me, but cutting into the Tube station I had lost him). Once through, I did my best to move quickly along the escalators and tunnels, losing my footing a number of times, bumping into others... shouts and curses in my direction.

Bakerloo line, for no other reason than that it was my first instinctual choice... Maybe, get as far as Waterloo, I could get on a real train! Make it to the Eurostar, and I'd lose the fuckers in Belgium!

Keep running... keep moving...

On the platform... southbound... Elephant & Castle, the rush of air and the high pitch of the brakes... nearly there...

Then something else: a distant shout... the echoed holler of panic and chaos from the tunnels behind me... something was coming...

The train stopped, the alarm of the doors sounded and the impatient exchange of passengers, those who want to leave and those who want to arrive... was that pounding the sound of my heart or the heavy rhythmic footfall of animal pursuit?

I jumped on the train and tried not to scream, shaking from top-to-toe, the drug and panic... Grabbing the hand-hold, I swung around to face the closing door and I swear the air rippled as *something* collided with the tube destination map, denting it, then turning towards the platform.

The train began to move, but as we left the platform the vague shimmer seemed to take form through the thick glass of the door-window and I had the short-lived impression of the beasts that were after me...

Bloody *hell*, but they were big...

tom

They just stood there... Waugh's 'men'... as Thackeray and I stared at them in turn, waiting for sign of movement, waiting for the atmosphere of this impasse to break.

"Do you think they will just leave?" Thackeray asked.

"No, not really... You?"

"No. They're just going to attack anyway, aren't they?"

"Yes... probably."

"Glad we both agree on that."

"Yeah..."

Waiting... There's nothing worse, is there?

Still... at least we had the comfort of knowing that Waugh was most likely having problems of his own right now...

waugh

I was smiling in that hard, truly thrilled manner, that can sometimes hurt your face after awhile. Think what you like, but there was an immense satisfaction in knowing that the bastards who had hurt my Richard had been dealt with so soundly.

Certainly my hounds must be hot on the heels of their prey by now — and I admit to wondering how many other lives they would take, loose on the London streets. Tonight would be a night of blood, and Richard deserved every drop.

Any moment now, my little puppets would drop all pretence of inaction and launch their violent ways on whoever was nearest; cold machines of tooth and nail. I was sure that the nightclub would be a field of carnage unequalled in recent local memory.

True, I had blown my lot in tonight's plans. No doubt few of the reanimates would return from the night's work, which left the reduced company of Yugo and I to rebuild from close to scratch. Still… I found I couldn't care less than I did. Maybe a short holiday, let the dust settle, then come back and start again… I had little enthusiasm for the work, but knew well enough that this was for the best. Start again, build bigger and stronger; not only for my sake, but also for the memory of a damned good friend…

I had parked in the small alley along from the club, thinking it best not to leave the car and its cargo in full view. As I turned the corner I removed my car keys and pressed the button that unlocked the doors. Maybe a month in Sardinia could be the ticket?

"Is this your car, Sir?" the man said; he and his colleague being lit-up briefly by the light of the orange indicators flashing a signal of my car's unlocking.

"And you are…?" It was all I could think of to say, the two men standing either side of me, both tensed against sudden movement on my part.

The man who had spoken removed his credentials from the inside pocket of his raincoat, "Detective Inspector Jarret, and my colleague here — the man that is about to press your face rather firmly against the bodywork of your vehicle — is Detective Constable Cottrell." I was shoved violently against the car, my nose giving a rather unpleasant popping sound as it collided with the roof. The keys were grabbed from my hand by the policeman and he dropped them in his pocket while pulling on a rubber glove and opening the rear door.

"We are very interested to ask you a few questions about the pair of corpses bleeding all over your upholstery. We received an… *anonymous* call which leads us to believe that you might prove fascinating company down at the station."

He looked at the body of Richard and the puppet. "Oh yes, I see that they were quite right. What a fascinating chat we all have ahead of us." He leaned into my vision and winked. "To put it in more professional terms, Mr. Waugh, I have the pleasure of informing you that 'you're *fucked*'."

max

They were in the tunnel... they must be. The only thing I needed to know *now* was how fast they could run. Surely we must be able to out-run them, barrelling along the tunnel as we were in this carriage...

Still they would follow, they knew where I was... but was that something I could use to my advantage? I tore off my jacket, ignoring the funny looks from my fellow passengers.

The train was quiet, thank God; an angry looking punk girl, who was trying her best to give the impression that I disgusted her, while also not caring whether I was near her or not (a tricky combo at the best of times); and a small Chinese man who was now paying a lot of attention to his book, though I'm sure that not a single word was sinking in. He didn't fool me.

The jacket wasn't enough, it wasn't my sweat they were following, it was my blood... I began to loosen the bandages on my arm, aware that time was against me, the train would be slowing for the next station any minute.

I leaned over to the punk and, with a deftness that I would have thought beyond me given my current condition, yanked the large safety pin from her canvas shoulder bag.

"Oi!" she shouted, an unsurprising touch of the Home Counties to her accent. It's always the posh birds, innit?

"Shush, you silly tart. When Rotten said 'No Future?', he was singing about me..." I replied, before really freaking her out by digging the pin into the wound in my arm and causing a thin stream of blood to run. In a way, the pain was good: it sharpened my mind through the fug of the Rebirth, and I kept digging to bring more blood down my arm and onto the jacket which I had scrunched in a ball and laid on the floor.

Max Jackson: Hunter / Adventurer had a plan...

I squeezed as much blood as I could onto the jacket and — just as the train pulled into Piccadilly Circus and the doors opened — I ran out as fast as I could towards the exit. Behind me, I could hear the sound of the doors closing and the train speeding off along its route. It would be a mistake to see if the things followed my trail, I decided. Either they would fall for it, in which case I had bought myself time; or they wouldn't, and I had just made a terrible mistake by sacrificing the advantage of speed.

Just keep running... time would iron out all questions soon enough.

I felt that I was starting to adapt to the drug in my system. Maybe it was the pain of messing with my arm wound, the adrenaline of panic, or even just the fact that I was getting used to the feeling. Don't get me wrong, I wasn't tempted to stop and do a soft-shoe shuffle next to the smelly old soak playing "Ruby Tuesday" on an out-of-tune guitar that

I ran past halfway to street level, but it was getting easier to think and move.

Another irritating fallacy to Tube transport is that 'it's fast'. This is a myth, promoted by the fact that the trains run every two or three minutes, making the sort of roar belting through the tunnels that makes you think the sound barrier is being softly nudged. Thing is, as it takes you half your journey time getting from platform to street, this hardly matters, does it? Up these stairs, along this corridor, up an escalator, along a bit, 'round and 'round you go... oh, here's another escalator... It's a complex labyrinth of tile and posters for movies and West End shows most Londoners will never see.

I was starting to lose hope of ever seeing daylight, when I finally emerged into the hustle and bustle of ticket barriers and the usual hordes of people desperate to be 'anywhere but here.'

I kept breathing slow, navigating both the crowd and the drug in my system and reached for the Oyster card in my jacket pocket... which turned out to be a bit of a problem of course, as I was no longer wearing the jacket which the pocket was a part of. I looked around and wondered 'exactly why it is that God has a habit of shitting on me so much...?' The place was swimming with staff, the barriers were all clunking closed with perfect functionality, and I couldn't for the life of me think how to get out without ending-up in a fist fight or a police cell. It seemed I had no option but to fall back on the most ridiculous act of human optimism.

"Excuse me, mate," I said to a large Rastafarian — whose colourful hat made my already questionable sight blur in the most alarming way — "some bastard's nicked my wallet and it had my ticket in it... I can't get out." Ingenious, yeah? I was willing to bet I was probably only the forty-eighth bloke that had tried to blag his way out with that excuse so far today.

He looked at me with bored resignation, recalling his official script for the situation. But he hadn't even begun to speak when I heard a ripple of shouts behind me. I turned around to see the crowd on the escalator looking over their shoulders at whatever it was that was causing such panic further down. I was afraid I could guess only too well...

"Do yourself a favour and run!", I shouted, pushing him out of the way and making a leap for the ticket barrier. Ignoring the angry shouts as I shoved people aside and threw myself over the gate, I landed badly on a floor made rough with the constant footfalls of a thousand Londoners. My arm spasmed as I thoughtlessly used it to push myself to my feet, then ran screaming towards the exit. I figured if I made enough noise, created a scary enough image, then people would get out of the way. If it's one thing that Londoners are trained for, its self-preservation. Behind me I heard a roar and couldn't resist looking back.

People were flying out of the way as something invisible forced its way past them in a bulk of sinew and claw. I could see wounds opening seemingly by themselves, as the creatures lashed out at the bodies between them and their prey. In a moment of horrible clarity, I watched a young woman scream as her chest was opened, sending an arc of blood spraying against the map of the Piccadilly line behind her, a new route formed between Leicester Square and Hell.

My head began pounding again — if anything stronger than before — and I ran out into the bustle of Piccadilly. Not only had I failed to give these things the slip, I had brought them to the one area of London that never goes quietly; even in the early hours, it's a mess of traffic and neon that screams 'buy me!' all through the night.

I ran wild, straight into the road and was knocked from my feet by a taxi cab that was pulling off at the lights.

'Watch it, dick-head!' the driver shouted, then looked away from me to the entrance of the tube station. I followed his gaze and saw the things properly for the first time, their hulking shape lit by the advertising hoardings and streetlights. I don't think he saw them, nobody did but me as far as I can tell. They responded to the weight of the things, or caught the panic as those close-by felt claws on their flesh, but Waugh was right: they seemed invisible to most.

There were two of them; each a grotesque realisation of the bulldogs from cartoons, great masses of gleaming muscle piled across their shoulders and upper torso, tapering away to a lithe pair of hind legs. Their head was little more than a rippling mouth to store their massive teeth in, the vague glint of second-hand light catching in a pair of small black eyes recessed away above a solid snout.

The image vanished again as they moved towards me and I pressed my hand against my pounding head and ran up Shaftesbury Avenue.

tom

Danny came through the doors just as I had been on the verge of getting Len to evacuate the club. For all I knew, the act of everybody clearing out might just have been enough to set Waugh's little army off, but it was getting to the point when anything was worth the risk. Surely they were likely to spring into action at any moment anyway, and while we only had a couple of security staff on the door — where was Douggie when you needed him? — I hoped that we might at least get some people to safety.

"I have no idea how long we've got", I said to Danny as he walked over. "The sound system's behind the bar."

He pulled his iPod from his pocket. "Lead the way, then."

I grabbed Len. "Help him connect the thing up, I wouldn't have the first idea."

"Is there anything I can do?" Thackeray asked, as I made for the stage.

"Find somewhere comfortable to sit down", I suggested, then stood up in front of the band who slowly stopped their rendition of Coltrane's *Lazy Bird* while looking at me with something approaching disgust. "Sorry gents, bit of an emergency," I said, and reached for the microphone.

"Ladies and gentlemen, sincere apologies for breaking the atmosphere, but I have a very important announcement to make." I looked to Waugh's men and my fist tightened around the mic as I saw them twitch, they were getting ready to attack... "Now Danny!" I shouted, a squeal of feedback making the room flinch as the speakers panicked at my raised voice...

A woman screamed as she was grabbed roughly from behind, a man raised his arms as the vacant reanimate next to him swung a punch in his direction... it was too late.

Then I blacked out.

max

I couldn't outrun them, that much was obvious. As I flailed my way along the lights of Shaftesbury Avenue, I desperately tried to think clearly enough to come up with a plan. I could hear the sound of emergency sirens in the distance. Someone had been on the blower, much good may it do them. Still, these things couldn't be *completely* invulnerable... could they...?

I swayed into the road, making a red Peugeot screech to a halt to avoid hitting me.

"What the hell are you doing?" the driver shouted, a ruddy looking man who had clearly had a couple too many to be behind the wheel. Good, he was on edge. Already expecting trouble.

I reached for my wallet and flipped it open in his direction. "Get out of the car please, Sir. We have reason to believe you are over the limit." I opened the door for him, desperate to keep him moving so that he didn't have time to question me.

"Hang on...", he said, one foot on the road and halfway out of the car. His speech was slurred; he really was too drunk to be driving and I doubt I'd have got him that far otherwise. He smiled as a penny dropped somewhere in his beer-soaked head. "Show me that i.d. again."

"Certainly, Sir." I smacked him in the face with all the strength I could muster, then thanked his piss-head gravity as it helped him fall out of the car and onto his back.

There was a growling sound behind me and I jumped into the driver's seat, engine still idling, and slammed the door shut.

"Get off my fucking car!", the drunk shouted, back on wobbly feet and banging at the window.

"Run, you silly bastard!", I shouted and slammed my foot on the accelerator.

I'm not a good driver, happy to admit it. Passed my test years ago, but I get behind the wheel so infrequently these days that it always feels like the first time again, and so I panic a little as I realise I might not quite know what I'm doing. It didn't matter right now, of course, I wasn't planning on setting any new safety standards, I just wanted something big and heavy to smack stuff with.

In the head lights I could see the pair of creatures stood side-by-side in the road, watching me cautiously. Like all animals, they had the good sense to suss out their lunch, making sure they didn't underestimate its ability to bite back. They were clever, they were strong and they were fast...

Luckily, not *that* fast...

The one to the left leaped towards the pavement. But that was okay,

I wasn't after him. The one on the right moved in the opposite direction, but I had been expecting it and swung the wheel so I broadsided the nasty bastard with all the weight a small French car can manage at about forty miles an hour. There was a loud crunch as the bonnet crumpled and the animal rolled up and over me, cracking the windscreen in a spider web as it went by.

The car stalled — well, yeah, *I* stalled it; told you I wasn't that good — and I struggled to turn the engine over again, then turned the car around so that I was facing the dogs.

The one that I had hit was dragging itself along the tarmac, so I had obviously done it a good bit of harm. The other was sidling at a distance, wary of taking me on. I over-revved the engine in nervousness, and went for another pass, hitting the wounded dog again as a gout of dark fluid that I took to be blood dowsed the broken windscreen. I gave a shout of rather pre-emptive joy, but kept my foot hard on the accelerator and aimed straight for the second one. It turned and began to run away from me up the road, knowing that it might not come off as well against me as it had thought, but I kept on its tail and — with speed and force entirely un-checked — slammed both it and the car into the wall of The Queen's Theatre.

I must have lost consciousness for a moment, as I had the experience of snapping awake with glass in my hair and a sharp pain in my midriff. I had broken a rib against the steering wheel; always in the bloody wars, me.

I opened the door and fell onto the pavement, the sound of sirens now damned loud. No great surprise. If you decide to get behind the wheel of a car and get in some hardcore demolition derby action in the heart of West End, you can expect to draw attention — especially if you pile said motor into the brickwork of one of the city's most famous theatres. Still, couldn't have been a better choice, in my humble opinion. I looked at the shattered hoarding that was advertising *Les Miserables* and couldn't help but smile a little. I fucking *hate* that show. I was thrown out once for giggling hysterically while the little kid gets shot...

I looked into the road for the dog I had hit twice, and there was a dark stain of blood and a mangled heap of flesh which, as I watched, faded from view. One definitely down. Now, if I was on form, then the other one should also be...

The car moved, shunted back on its knackered wheels... the dog was far from dead and pushing its way out of the wreckage.

Bollocks.

Limping now, having to contend with yet more physical injury on top of the Rebirth — which may even have been doing me a favour by now, keeping my system rocketing along when, by all rights, it should have just closed down and given up — I gave a moan and went on the run again.

danny

If there's one thing that I consider a genuine fuck-up that night, it was my only bringing one extra pair of ear-plugs. Have you any idea how much hard work it is for two men to carry thirty prone bodies into a bar cellar?

"I intend to ask that little sod for a substantial pay rise", Len, the manager, wheezed as we dropped the last of Waugh's boys down the hatch behind the bar. "Do you by any chance have something in that music collection of yours to make alcoholic club owners hand over all their worldly goods to abused members of staff?"

I looked around the club, making sure that we hadn't missed anyone. It was hard to tell, and without Len's eye for his customers I wouldn't have known where to start. The whole room was a mass of unconscious people: heads lolling, limbs splayed over the tables, and a fair few out for the count in the middle of the floor where they had been *en route* to the bar or toilets when I had pressed PLAY on the sound wave that had knocked them out. "I'll see what I can find, maybe program in a free bar tab for myself while I'm at it."

Len smiled, his bushy moustache rippling (I had no idea anyone wore one of those these days, he looked like a refugee from the seventies or a German beer seller). "For once I'd even turn a blind eye to it;" he said, "you've more than earned it." He poured us both a drink. Decent Scotch. Good man. "I suppose we'd better make this lot a bit more presentable too. It's going to be difficult enough without having to explain to some irate customer why he's suddenly found himself face down in a decorative pot plant. How long will this thing last?', he pointed towards the iPod.

"They could be out all night if I wanted, it's potent stuff. If I don't play the reversal wave they would be stone cold for hours."

"That might be pushing our luck too far," he said, "but at least we've time for another drink." He topped up our glasses and we clashed them together in a toast.

max

"All I wanted was a couple of quid!", the addict shouted, just before the remaining dog bit his face off.

I had run as far as I could, weaving off the main strip, trying to lose the animal in the alleys and side streets that fill the gap between London's main thoroughfares. It was slower than before: I may not have killed it with the car but I had obviously damaged it, otherwise it would have caught-up with me long before now.

Then I had to run into this poor bastard: lose my momentum, lose my head-start.

I pulled myself along the surface of the road, wondering for a moment whether it was worth calling for help. The street had a few cars parked along it, four or five, all worth money (you didn't get to live this close to the action without having a few pounds in the bank). I realised there was little point, all it was likely to do was put someone else's death on my conscience. That wasn't fair, for them or me.

I rolled onto my back and pushed myself upon my elbows, watching as the creature flung the homeless man to one side and slowly padded towards me.

I said earlier on that one of the greatest mysteries reanimates face is knowing what happens after they have completely fallen apart. Do they — as looks likely — still hold on to sentience? Mind and awareness trapped in rotting, sundered flesh? Or are they cast loose, perhaps? Bodiless and an infinity of mental wandering? Or, maybe, if you did the body enough damage, do we finally get to just die? Turn off? Flip the switch and experience no more?

It looked like I was about to find out. Sure as hell there wouldn't be much left of me once this bastard had had its fill.

There was a flash of movement behind it, just at the mouth of the street. I caught it out of the corner of my eye and it only really registered because it seemed familiar to me.

The dog halted, sensing something amiss with one of its sharp animal senses.

All along the street, one by one, the parked car's headlights flashed on, lighting us up as surely as theatre footlights. I pulled myself further back from the beast — still on my elbows, still watching — as the dog turned to see what was going on. Scuffling as far as I could from the thing while it was distracted, I put another few feet between us before I collapsed again and couldn't move any further. I looked to see what was happening.

What I saw, just past its bulky shoulder seems ridiculous but then, doesn't most of my life?

Mattie was walking towards us, casual and slow. He had that

wonderful rolling gait which cats have as the muscles ripple from their back legs, along their spine, and then to the front. Cats strut like Travolta at the end of *Staying Alive*... cool bastards they are. As he passed each car, its engine roared into life; yet he didn't acknowledge them, didn't look to either side, he kept his eyes fixed on the dog. He arched his back slightly, making himself look bigger, mad sod... as if it was going to hold much weight with this thing! How the hell had he found me? I felt a surge of immense sadness, this silly little thing had tracked me down somehow and was now just as much in line for an evisceration as I was. It seemed so unfair, hardly sound payment for its impressive act of hunting.

Still... the cars roared where they stood. How did he do that?

The dog growled deep in its throat, Mattie replied, low and threatening.

The dog tensed to pounce, to tear this ridiculous beast apart and get back to the main course.

Mattie howled! Fangs bared, mouth wide, ears flat against his beautiful black and white head, the air filled with the roaring of car engines.

The dog jumped towards him and the front car — a Mercedes, no less — left the ground and thrust at the beast mid-air, smacking it back against the wall to the left of us in a squeal of tearing metal and a howling burglar alarm. The second car came flying — one of the BMW 3 series — soft top whipping away to hang behind it like a cape, as it dived nose-first into the mess of dog and Mercedes.

Mattie hopped on all fours, doing that sideways dance that cats do in a fight, springing like Ali... sting like a bee!

The wall crumbled, the torn rear end of the creature twitching and pumping that dark blood which ran through its veins, while the pile of car and bricks fell to the ground. It lay still... finally... dead.

I fell fully onto my back, exhaustion and the impossibility of my night weighing down on me, as Mattie walked towards me. In the distance of my hearing, I heard a car screeching to a halt and someone shouting my name.

Mattie walked up my body and sat down on my chest, purring. It was the drug — obviously, I'm not that mad — but I swear the last thing I heard before losing consciousness completely was a small yet rich voice in my head...

Hungry. More tuna. Now.

tom

1.

It's a wonder to me sometimes that I still have a club to run. What with bar brawls and the entire *clientèle* baffled as to how they seem to have lost a chunk of the evening.

When Danny woke us all up, I found myself sat on a bar stool in front of a baffled room full of people who knew on a subconscious level that something extremely strange had just happened. The sound wave was instant and there was no sense of slipping in and out: one minute I had been stood up shouting into a microphone, the next I was sat down and looking as gormless as everybody else. Still... the sense of absence was strong and you could tell the whole club was severely disorientated. Call me a professional, but I sprang to the rescue with considerable aplomb:

"Free bar for the next ten minutes!" and then I made a mad dash from the stage determined to beat the rush.

2.

Dave managed to catch up with Max — and Jerusalem's ex-cat for some bloody reason — the trail of damage proving easy enough to follow for one of even his fairly limited intelligence. He carried Max into the bar — the cat padding along at their heels — and walked straight through to my office where Thackeray, Danny, Len and I joined them.

Max told us all what had happened and I admit to assuming he'd beefed it up a little. Not that I'm calling Max a liar, so much as a natural storyteller; there's a big difference.

Having said that, there *were* plenty of items on the news to back up many of his claims. In that wonderful way that 'the powers that be' have, the whole thing ended up being written off as a 'terrorist attack' — a neat if rather preposterous cover — which stuck despite some of the more outlandish witness reports in the tabloids for days after.

I didn't care. Max was fine (well, as fine as he often is anyway, nothing a bit of attention from Thackeray and several weeks of whinging wouldn't cure) that was the main thing.

Once he was sure Max was fine, Thackeray was on the phone to his friends in the police and checking on Waugh. Underhanded and simple it may have been, but it seemed to have solved the immediate problem. There wasn't much likelihood of him being back about his business in anything like the near future. The police had found a knife in the glove-box with Waugh's fingerprints on the handle, plus a plenty of blood belonging to the corpses in his car upon its blade. It might not be quite open-and-shut, but it's close enough once a few strings were pulled and words whispered in the right legal circles.

Let's say 'open, scratch your chin for a few seconds, *then* shut', shall we?

I don't feel it was punishment enough for what he did, but sometimes you just have to make do. There was no doubt that we had got ourselves involved in a mess way beyond our ability to deal with, and I know that we all considered ourselves bloody lucky to have got out of it with our beautiful skins intact.

Loose ends? Yeah... plenty of them.

I had a cellar full of reanimates to deal with for a start. Thackeray ended up re-homing them like unwanted Christmas puppies. They are now staring at the walls of spare bedrooms dotted about the city, looked after by those among our community who had the sensitivity and money to do so. I think of them a lot, we all do. 'There but for the grace of God' springs to mind, lost souls bouncing around their own empty skulls.

I kept one guy, Mark Ford according to his driving license, and am trying to do my best by him. He sleeps here at the club, helps change barrels, clean up; mundane jobs, but I struggle to teach him anything else. Some nights, when the punters have gone home and we're getting straight before calling it a night, I watch him push his brush slowly along the floor, catching fag ends and spilt trash. Sometimes he just stops and stares into space. I hunt for meaning in his eyes, is he remembering his old life? Has a spark of awareness lit-up that wounded mind, if only for a second?

I'm still waiting for a sign of it. Waiting and hoping.

waugh

Prison is not impossible to endure. Wilde managed, as did de Sade. I have no intention of not following their example.

My fellow inmates leave me alone for the most part; one positive to being wrongly convicted of such violent murder is that one is seen as being more than capable of handling oneself. I have let the reputation stand: it would be no use to protest my innocence, and in the long run it's better that people believe me more than capable of such acts.

Richard would be proud, for I have learned from his example of how to be perceived by the mob: I am a dangerous man and nobody has any inclination to test the fact.

I have considerable time to be able to pursue my studies too, and I must say that the government's reforms for prisons and the enviable access to information I have both through the internet and the library — who will order me any title I wish for — are most appreciated.

Yes, it's a quiet life, interrupted only occasionally by my loyal visitor.

"My darling Aycliffe; good to see you, as always! How is Yugo?"

The young man has been visiting me every week, as good as gold. He comes with his little notebook and his open mind and, soon, we may even start to see some semblance of normality return to business...

After all, I see no reason why this incarceration should be anything but an irritating imposition on the growth of my empire. One can control from a distance — it's slow, true — and I have so much to try and teach the boy. But he's intelligent and ambitious, therefore I have no doubt that I shall see things improving soon enough.

next on Deadbeat...

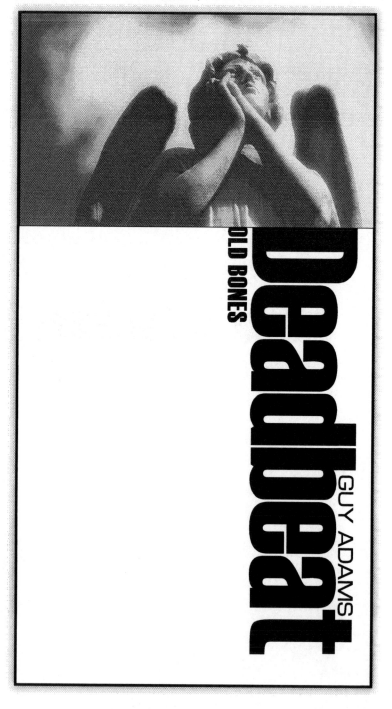

Deadbeat
OLD BONES

1.

The early hours roll over suburban streets, the only noise being the distant buzz of traffic from the M25: a road that never sleeps, there's always someone wanting to escape the city. Between the houses a churchyard waits, knowing in the fabric of its overlong grass verges and exhaust-stained headstones that it will see action tonight.

A mile or so away, and life can still be found. The centre of Richmond is well-lit and peppered with late-night drinkers and graveyard shift workers stumbling to or from the warmth of their beds. A boy — too young for life on the streets — crumbles stray tobacco from dog-ends into a crumpled Golden-Virginia pouch that's seen long service in the stained pocket of his jeans. He will roll the un-smoked leaves again while waiting for sleep in the doorway of the dry-cleaners where he's made his bed for the night. Sometimes he dreams of a childhood in the North, sometimes he sleeps easy.

Anastazy Zaleski rides his twin-brushed vehicle along the pavements, sucking up the shit of yet another day. He does this with a smile; the work is easy and the pay more than he could get back home. His mind wanders as the engine lulls him, dreaming of pretty English girls and a cottage in the country. He knows he will never have them, but dreaming is enough.

Stacey Bradley shuffles home with a head full of Ibsen and a thigh damp from the leaked attentions of the small-time director who has just cast her in his production. She wistfully searches the night sky for imagined hawks, the ghost of verse on her lips and a dream of rapt audiences in her mind. She narrowly misses being run-over by a navy transit van, and stumbles onto the pavement landing back in the real world and away from Norwegian mountains.

"Careful, you mad bastard!", she shouts, but the vehicle drives on obliviously, towards the silent residential streets of the suburbs and the graveyard still patiently waiting.

2.

The terraced rows of dreamers that surround *St. Mary's of the Annunciate* have no interest in the salvation offered by its billboard posters. "What's missing from this Ch__ch?" asks one in day-glo pink. Another invites all to a discussion of the importance of faith in the modern world. "God Willing!" is scrawled in the corner, seeming less a play on words and more a churlish caveat. Perhaps God will be busy that day; certainly most of the populace will, England are playing Chile on Sky Sports and unless God is willing to offer free beer and a wides-creen telly there will be few takers.

A navy transit pulls up against the lych-gate, which looked out over fields before progress surrounded it with brick and roads. BANG and the peace of this small suburban hour is shattered by the slamming of the van door and the thud of heavy-soled boots.

"Announce it to the whole street why don't you?", the driver hisses.

"Sorry, Jeff, lost my grip on the handle."

"Lost your fucking grip alright, we're supposed to be a stealth team! Come on."

Stealth team? Mark Chad isn't altogether sure what one of those is. Stealth wasn't a prerequisite in the Butcher's trade, the animals were dead by the time they arrived in his chiller, he didn't have to sneak up on them. But then that had been back when life was normal, back before the accident that had killed him. These days he was someone else entirely (although he still kept his cleaver hand busy, even the dead liked their sausages). Jeff – nobody knows his second name, militant and edgy, he hangs onto his anonymity like a security blanket – zips up his jacket and pulls his balaclava down over his face. Mark refuses to wear his — it makes his cheeks itch — but Jeff is rarely seen without it, he had to be convinced to peel it back while driving as they had all agreed it was far more suspicious and likely to draw attention. Jeff loves the secret squirrel stuff... makes him feel important.

The third in the team, a one-time surveyor from Cardiff, clambers out of the back carrying the equipment.

""Sorry Rhys," Mark whispers, "want a hand?"

"Wouldn't bloody mind, I'll be arse-over-tit in a minute otherwise."

Mark grabs the tall kit bag, being careful not to let the spade blades bash together for fear of another dressing-down from Jeff who is already pacing around the churchyard, checking for non-existent danger.

"Look at him," Rhys mutters, "he's such a wanker."

"Corporal Jeff?", Mark grins, poking fun at the man's military pretensions. "His heart's in the right place, you'll get used to him.'

Rhys hadn't been with them for long. They'd got chatting over a pint a fortnight ago and he'd decided to join up, feeling that he might be of some use. In truth, he had been invaluable, as his knowledge of electronics had given them a technological boost which meant they might actually get somewhere after months of wasted gallivanting and arguing..

He bundles the mess of wires and headphones under his arm and props a short pole over his shoulder, "Come on then, let's get on with it."

They huddle down in the shadow of the church wall while Rhys connects-up his equipment: a rough but functional thing, cobbled together from eBay and electronic catalogues. The pole was salvaged from a metal detector, but the circular pad at its base didn't register electromagnetics anymore, it was tuned very differently.

"Ready?", Jeff asks impatiently.

Rhys puts the headphones on his head and nods. "I am wired for sound!"

Mark chuckles and he and Rhys begin humming Cliff Richard.

"Knock it off!", Jeff whispers. "let's start a sweep."

Rhys and Mark roll their eyes, but shut up nonetheless and start to work their way along the grass paths of the churchyard.

"This is silly," Mark mutters after ten minutes or so. "Most of these buggers have been in the ground for decades."

"Over here!", Jeff calls, looking around in case any 'hostiles' might have heard his raised voice.

The two men stroll over to him and Jeff points at the ground "Two months old, worth a go."

Rhys sighs and points his sensor at the earth. "Not a sausage." Which doesn't surprise him in the least, after twelve jaunts around midnight, they've come away empty-handed every time. Given the odds, it wouldn't surprise him if they *never* found what they were looking for.

Then something crunches in his ear. "Wait… stand still a minute…' He points the directional mic more carefully, making sure he doesn't brush it against the grass or dead leaves.

The three of them freeze, a gentle breeze wafting through the tombstones the only thing that moves.

"Well…?", Jeff asks after a few seconds.

"Hang on," Rhys whisperes impatiently, "I want to be sure."

He tries to blank-out everything else and focus on the quiet rhythm in his ears. Now that he comes to it, he realizes he is terrified by the idea of actually finding what they had set out for, and frightened even more by the possibility of mis-reading the information.

"What do you reckon," Mark asks, "have we got one?"

Rhys draws breath, trying to gather a little courage now it has actually come to the crunch. "Bugger me, but I think we have."

The three of them look at one another and Jeff's balaclava suddenly rumples against a huge grin, "Crack the spades out, lads: let's get digging!"

3.

None of them are quite prepared for how back-breaking the digging will be. It always looked a lot easier in the movies — but then, Mark realises, they usually cut away from the hard work — which made it seem like the matter of moments to shift several feet of earth and sod. Jeff even takes his balaclava off as it is making him sweat too much.

Eventually though Mark scrapes the lid of the coffin with his spade. "Got it!"

"Quick, find the edges!" Jeff says and they all drop to the ground scooping the remaining earth away more carefully. Another few minutes sees all three men staring down at a slightly warped wooden casket lid and wondering if they could really go through with what comes next. Even Jeff seems to be struggling to find his bottle now. "Are you sure?", he asks Rhys.

"Of course I'm not, but it sounded right, like the practice. What do you want me to say? I'm as positive as I ever could be."

They look at one another again, Mark remembering the hysteria in his front room when they'd first tested Rhys' scanner. He had lain under a pile of sofa cushions while the Welshman pointed the microphone at him from the top of a stepladder. It had been a laugh then, three mates pissing about with a few beers and a silly idea. Now it was almost too much for him to stand.

A cat howls from a few houses away and all three flinch in panic. "For fuck's sake", Mark hisses. "This is getting stupid." Then — as much to have it all over as anything else — he rams the point of his crowbar at the rim of the coffin and starts to wrench it open.

All three set to it. They are as quiet as possible, but, after two months of being pressed down by earth, weathered by drained rainwater and the pale white creatures that make their home in the soil, it takes considerable work to crack the lid open. When the wood finally splinters and gives way, it is with a sharp crack that they all ignore, just desperate to have it finished and be on their way.

Inside the coffin, lit by the pale grey of a half moon, a woman lies in crumpled white. Her face is sunken, cheek bones prominent like the starvation victims you see on the news and charity adverts. Her hair is a mess of black shadow, splayed around her sickly face like the wafting fronds of a sea anemone. She is quite still. Rhys sticks out his hand to touch her only to snatch it away before making contact, scared of the feel of cold, dead flesh.

"Shit", Jeff whispers. "I think we've really fucked up here."

She opens her eyes.

All three fall back from the hole in the ground, scrabbling in the piles of earth that they had dumped to either side.

Much to his surprise, it is Mark that actually gets it together first, crawling back over to the hole and smiling down at the woman. She is still un-moving, but her face shows a terror to match his own, which makes him feel a little easier.

'Hello," he says, glancing at her headstone for her name, "*Emily*. We've come to rescue you."

to be continued...

Deadbeat: Old Bones
by Guy Adams

ISBN 978-1-905532-21-6

available at www.humdrumming.co.uk
and through all better bookstores

Special Features:
"EARTH"

I woke up this morning to find a woman in my bed and I still don't know what to do about it. At the time, I slipped out from under my side of the duvet and crept out of the room, not willing to make any decisions just yet. Besides, I had work to do — make a few calls, y'know, the usual.

I was on the street by ten: cold air and crowded pavements. Everywhere you went, the lampposts and shop fronts were draped with lights and tinsel. Each store you went into was playing the same CD — Roy Wood was wishing it could be Christmas everyday over and over again. The shop assistants wore smiles as freshly minted as the cash that flowed through their hands. People fought, laughed, cried. Children yelled. Car horns barked. Come eleven, I was hiding out in a coffee shop wishing the World would have the decency to shut its damned mouth for a second. Just enough to give me room to breathe.

And all the while, thinking about that woman lying in my bed.

Christmas is a crazy time for me; business gets kind of weird. A lot of my regulars drop off the radar for a while, bitten by the Jesus bug. Guilt and a newfound sense of religious propriety make them lie low. They'd be back of course. Nobody dropped out forever, just wait until January had crushed all the soul out of them; the phone would ring soon enough.

Christmas also brought me new faces, those that would never normally score. This time of the year just gets to some people, people sick of all that 'good living family' bullshit being rammed down their throats at every possible opportunity. You can only take so much perfection being thrown at you; after a bit, it begins to feel like someone's laughing at you. That's when they come to me.

I can give them something to make them better, to fill a hole in themselves or put one in someone else. That's what I do.

I deal in magick.

Nothing major as a rule — though I've dabbled in some heavy stuff from time to time — just the usual boring clichés. Love spells, curses, uppers and downers. Your basic Urban *Voudoun*. Incantation stuff.

I also sell a few charms, texts, objects of 'power', all that hokey rigmarole.

What can I say? It keeps the roof over my head.

I finished my coffee and headed up west where I was due to meet a client at half eleven. His name's Jeff (I don't swap surnames, most of my clients like to feel there's a bit of anonymity), works in advertising or some other soul-sapping crap. Decent guy, for an office monkey anyway. He doesn't play with the big stuff, always pays cash: bread and butter, in other words.

I met him at a little Sushi place across the road from his office. One of those chrome and plastic seat affairs, low comfort — high price.

"Hi Danny," he said, strolling through the door with some other guy I've never met. If anyone else had tried this with me they'd have been handed their brain on one of the little sushi plates that revolve around the counter. You had to be careful in my line of business. Still Jeff was no idiot, if he thought the guy was safe, then he probably was.

"...Jeff. Who's your friend?"

"This is Tommy, works across the way from me. Thought you might be able to fix him up with some stuff."

"Yeah?" I shuffled in my seat a little. Trust or no trust, this wasn't how I liked to do business. I pointed at the couple of seats facing mine. "Well then, keep your voice down and park yourselves. What sort of stuff are we talking about here?"

Tommy was middle aged, his gut pressing at his shirt buttons from the inside. Hair was thinning, forehead shiny. He kept rubbing his hands together though through nervousness or excitement I couldn't really tell. Both probably.

"He's got a thing about one of the girls in accounts..." Jeff said, chuckling like a schoolboy.

"He can tell me himself, can't you Tommy?" I went to light a cigarette, then remembered that such pleasures were now forbidden in public (as so many really pleasurable things are), and just fidgeted with the pack.

Tommy sighed and looked around to see if anyone was watching us. They weren't. For all my moaning about Jeff mouthing off, I'm not stupid: I'd placed a discretion charm around the table before they even came in. Anyone listening wouldn't pick up a word.

"It's like Jeff says, Tina's her name."

"Okay. What exactly is it you want from me?"

"I just want something to make her like me."

I sighed, one day somebody will sing a different song but for now it was all the usual melody.

"I can't *make* her like you, Tommy, not really. I can make her *think* she likes you, but that really isn't the same thing is it? You sure you know what you're doing with this?"

He looked at me then and I could see in his vacant little pig eyes that he knew damn well what he wanted. Christ, for all their talk of 'love' or 'like', it always boils down to the same thing. They just want to get their end away without recrimination; the magickal form of Rohypnol.

Which made me think of the woman in my bed.

Which, in turn, took all the fight out of me.

Hell, let 'em do what they want.

"Yeah, I can fix you up. It won't be cheap, but it'll get you what you want. I'm going to need some stuff from you though, I'll do you a list."

I scribbled in the little notebook I always carried. All the usual mythic crap: lock of hair, recent photo... You know the sort of thing.

"What about you Jeff? The usual, is it?"

Jeff was your common or garden variety esteem junkie, the other best seller in my stock. I sold him a small charm that he wore around his neck, it doesn't make people like him but it sure as hell makes him like himself — which tends to lead to the same thing in the end doesn't it? In all fairness, I was running a bit of a con on Jeff though: the charm worked, that was fine but I had him under the impression that it needed replacing every couple of months — just to keep the sales up, y'know? Kind of dirty I'll admit, but he can afford it. Besides, it makes y the thing seem more potent somehow, as if it's kicking out a lot of juice.

"Yeah, thanks pal." He winked and passed me a thick envelope, which I swapped for one from my own pocket.

Nice and smooth. I turned to Tommy.

"Once you get everything on my shopping list, you give me a call and I'll see what I can sort out."

"Okay, thanks"

"Don't thank me until I've done something to earn it."

I got to my feet.

"Wait a minute," Jeff said, pulling another envelope from his pocket. "This is for you."

I took it and tore it open. Inside there was a Christmas card. One of those arty minimalist affairs, black-and-white close-up of a holly leaf or some shit. I threw it on the table.

"I'm not your friend Jeff. Save it for someone who is."

The poor bastard was stunned, and I felt a pang of guilt as I walked out. Truth is, he'd caught me on a tender subject. I don't do Christmas. Hate it. I'm one of those bitter people I mentioned earlier. Not that he could have known that.

I nearly walked back in to apologize, but I was still feeling angry and decided I'd only screw it up. Hell with it: I'd call him later.

I walked around the block a couple of times, just to calm down and then rang my next client. 'Joe the Taxi' he calls himself. Guess he must have liked the song. He really is a cab driver though, which is pretty damned useful at times. He gives me a lift to where I need to be and we conduct our business at the same time.

It took him about ten minutes to get over to me, during which I smoked a cigarette and tried to decide what to do about the woman in my flat. I was still none the wiser as I climbed into the back of his cab and gave him the directions.

"How's it going Danny?" he asked as we made our way along all the little side streets and back alleys that you only ever see from the back of a cab. God help you if you ever try to find them on your own, you'll be lost within seconds. This is Cabbie Magic.

"Yeah... bad time of year, Joe. You know how it is."

"Caroline, yeah?"

"Yeah."

Joe knew all about Caroline. When I'd got the call he was the one that ran me to the hospital. Double quick time too I have to say... not that it did any good: she was dead on arrival. Not many people walk away from the wrong end of a drunk in a Mercedes and Caroline was no exception. That had been two Christmases ago. Which would be why I lack a certain 'seasonal spirit'.

"It's tough, Danny, I know."

He did too, though his wife was still alive, just living in Birmingham with an Optician and their two kids. I thought about telling him what had happened that morning (he was as close as I got to a friend these days). I decided not to though, at least not until I knew what I was going to do about it.

"How about you, Joe? What can I do you for?"

"Ah... just a bit more Karkash Root, my supplies getting kind of low."

"No problem." I'd guessed as much and had brought a half-pound with me on the off chance.

Joe's got any interesting solution to the loneliness thing, you see: he builds *homunculi*. They look like women, move like women, feel like women... Difference is they're not real; just dummies — dolls. The Karkash Root comes in from West Africa; it's the base ingredient in giving the things an appearance of life.

I'll be honest: I've tried it, but it really didn't work out. They have a lifeless look in their eyes that freaks me out. That and the idea of them just falling apart after a few weeks. It's good for Joe though: he can't bear the idea of starting again, he hasn't the confidence. At least this way he can feel like there's somebody around, someone to care for him.

I dumped the package on his passenger seat as we pulled up.

"Call it a present." I said.

"Hey, are you sure?"

"Yeah, don't worry about it."

"Thanks. Look after yourself, okay?"

I smiled — though I'll admit it was forced — and waved him off.

I strolled down the street a little way, grabbing another smoke. I was going to make Billy the last call of the day — I really did have to sort the situation out back home — but I always made sure I arrived a little late for this one. It didn't pay to have him think I needed him too much. See, Billy was my supplier — one of them anyway. I know some stuff — I'm a fair Magus on an everyday level — but when it comes to more specialist requirements, I give Billy a call. He's a bit of a theatrical prick — swans about the place in a caftan reeking of incense — and he will try and convince you he's part of a long *Houngan* line from Haiti, whereas I have it on good authority he's a Brixton boy through and through. There's no denying he knows his subject though, and for any stuff I need but don't want to get too involved in, he's my best contact.

I paused outside a flower shop while I finished my cigarette. There was a large bunch of white lilies in the window. Caroline had always loved lilies. I used to buy her a bunch every now and then, not as often as I should have I'm sure, but y'know — 'regularly'.

The last time I'd bought some for her was when they put her in the ground.

I dropped my cigarette and trod on it before walking past a few more houses and up to Billy's front door.

I rang the bell and pulled at my coat, Christ but it was getting cold out here.

Billy opened the door and the wave of Patchouli that hit me in the face nearly had me throwing up on his front step.

"Ah…" his voice rumbled, "Danny, my son, it is good to see you."

"Yeah, you too. Billy. Let me in, would you? I'm freezing out here."

He stepped out of the way so that I could get inside. It was still something of a struggle; Billy's a big man. Likes his cakes.

I shuffled through to his front room and took a seat on his sofa.

"Get you a drink, Danny?"

"Yeah, whatever's going."

I started to warm up, he had the gas fire up on full and, despite the skulls and horns he had hanging everywhere, I was getting quite comfy as he passed me a beer.

"So," he said, dropping into a reclining armchair with a crash, "how did it go?"

"…What?" I asked.

"The thing, last week, the incantation."

"Oh, come on," I said sipping at my beer, "You know I'm not a user, I passed that on and I've had no complaints."

He looked at me for a few moments.

"Not a user huh?"

"Damn right, I strictly deal — you know that."

He took a drink of his beer and nodded.

"Whatever you say, Danny, whatever you say."

I was tensing up, hadn't been expecting this. I'd just wanted to place a couple of big orders and then get home. I needed to get home…

(Because there was a woman in my bed and I didn't know what to do about it)

…and keep my head down until the World got over this stupid Christmas thing and we could all get on with business as normal.

He looked at me again and I could tell he was weighing up whether to push the subject. Eventually he just nodded again and took another mouthful of beer.

"So, what can I get for you?"

I took out my notepad and reeled off a few orders I'd taken over the last couple of days, glad to just get the business over and done with. He made a few notes of his own and finished his beer.

"You want another one?" he asked.

I did, but not here.

"I'm fine, I've got to be getting on — few more things to do before everybody vanishes for a couple of days."

"Yeah, know what you mean. Okay, I'll give you a call when I can fix you up."

"Great." I got to my feet and he led me back to the front door.

"Danny?" he said as I was walking down his path, shivering against the sudden drop in temperature.

"Yeah?" I turned to look at him, hands in my coat pockets, shoulders hunched.

"Make sure you know what you're doing."

I was going to question him, demand to know what he meant — I hate all that enigmatic crap he throws about, that sort of thing's for the punters not me — but he closed the door before I had chance. I stayed there for a moment, just stood on his path, then swore under my breath and headed back along the street.

The shop windows were trying to convince me it was a good time of the year: posters for greetings cards, twinkling fairy lights, great tubs of wrapping paper and spinning baubles. I didn't believe them.

I was about to call a cab when I saw the neon of a small bar. A quick drink would do me good, I felt. Just a little more breathing space before I had to go home.

It turned out to be several and the sky was beginning to get dark by the time I stumbled out.

I called my cab and strolled up and down the street while I waited, trying to decide what to do.

When the car came I was feeling a lot better, more resolved. It was understandable that I'd been nervous; it'd been two years, for God's sake. Still, sometimes you've just got to do it haven't you?

By the time I stepped in through my flat door it was dark, the flashing Christmas lights from the street outside pulsing through my windows and throwing their red, orange and green across my walls.

There's a woman in my bed.

I went to flick on the hall light then drew short. It was so quiet, had she gone? Left me? Had I offended her by dashing out this morning?

I walked through to the bedroom and paused in the doorway as the second hand lights from outside lit up the shape in bed. She was still here. Still in my bed.

I walked slowly towards her holding out the Lilies I'd dashed back to the shop for while waiting for my taxi.

"Merry Christmas love", I said, surprised at how natural the words sounded.

The shape moved and sat up in bed, a pulse of red catching the side of her face. She was a bit of a mess, hair splayed about her face. Still, I'd expected it, Billy had warned me about that.

I sat on the bed and held the flowers out to her. When she didn't take them, I just laid them her lap.

"Lilies, love, your favourite."

She didn't say anything; did she even remember?

"Caroline, love, remember? Lilies?"

"Lilies?" she whispered, her voice rough and dry.

"That's right!"

And I took her in my arms and kissed her, inhaling deep the musty smell of earth.

Special Features:
AUTHOR'S COMMENTARY

1.

The author rests with his arse suspended in the air between two Captain's chairs, with the fug of stale cigarette smoke and cheap gin wafting around the recording booth. His headphones are skew-whiff, covering one eye with the cord wrapped around his lower face.

There is a loud whine of feedback as the recording engineer turns on the radio between his desk and the booth.

"Wake up you ridiculous sod! Book Two!"

Adams falls off his stool with a moan and a whining fart, before crawling back into some semblance of professionalism.

"Right... Book Two... yeah... sorry, I'd given up on it to be honest."

"You're not the only one. Now get one with it..."

2.

Yeah... bit of a gap that, wasn't it? Sorry about that.

This book was scheduled to be released last summer (2006 for those arriving at the party late) and then pushed back to September for **FantasyCon** (also 2006), as both work on a 'tie-in' book for the television series *Life On Mars* and emigrating to Spain meant that I hadn't had time to write much more than the preview that was included in the re-issue of the first book, *Makes You Stronger*.

I ended up defaulting on that deadline too, as the business of earning a living as a writer — it was a hobby when I wrote the first book, but it's a job now — kept meaning that I had to set priority for the paying gigs and push *Deadbeat* back again (don't get me wrong: I write because I love it, these books especially, but I don't think anybody would be surprised were I to say that neither I nor Humdrumming get rich doing what we do — often the opposite).

Couldn't be helped, there's only so many hours in the day and I had also gone from being a bachelor with all the late nights and spare time that such a state allows, to being a fiancé with two step-kids and a mortgage to help pay.

Life changes doesn't it? Oh yes...

There was also a part of me that wanted to let a bit of water flow before Humdrumming released another book with my name on it. It's no secret that I'm a big part of the company — tough not to be, when there are only *three* of us! — and I was wary of opening myself up any further to accusations of nepotism.

When we originally launched the company, we needed books quickly and so two of them were by me. Even though I had published *The Imagineer* under a pseudonym, it was the work of moments to find the original, out of print edition on Amazon and link the real me to it, and an even easier job once *More Than This* was released a few months later under my own name (yet featuring the pseudonymous Gregory Ashe as a main character!). I don't regret having those books go out through a company I had a vested interest in. It makes a lot of sense in fact, as I still own the copyright on all three lock, stock and barrel, plus have complete control over what happens to them. Still, I admit it felt uncomfortable — still does a bit, even though I hope the reviews show that they were worth putting into readers hands — so I decided a few months ago that the *Deadbeat* series will be the only books I continue to release through the company so as to completely separate myself from the worry! We're a fragile bunch, we writers; these things bother us…

Anyway, finally I found the time, hope you liked it as much as the first one…

A bit thigh-slapping in the end perhaps, with Waugh in classic 'I will return!' *Fu-Manchu* mode, but Hell, I liked him and wanted to keep him. This is a book where we have a demolition derby in Shaftesbury Avenue and a small cat saves the day… it ain't Shakespeare, is it?

He was *much* sillier.

3.

I love cats. They love me. Works out well.

When I met my fiancée Debra, she and her sons Joe and Dan had three cats. Brian (an old tabby who sadly died of being extremely ancient just before we emigrated last year), Mango, and Mattie.

Mattie was a wonderful, spirited, naughty, black and white mass of lithe bad behaviour. He was playful as well as surprisingly sentimental. You couldn't not love him.

Unless you hate cats, of course; in which case please send me your address and I will come 'round and do bad things to your lawn.

At the time, I was living just across the road from Debs and the boys, and work meant early mornings so I would be in bed by half-ten or so, bouncing between her house and my flat depending on shifts and inclination. One day, Mattie moved in with me. He followed me home one night and fell asleep on the pillow next to my head. If he wasn't there when I went to sleep, he certainly would be by morning, having snuck in via an old cat-flap that still sat next to the front door from some long-forgotten feline of tenants past.

Dan was a little upset to begin with, as Mattie had been his cat, but he knew well enough that cats make their own decisions and you can't force them into anything. Mattie was a cat who liked attention and he preferred living with me in my flat where there weren't other animals to share the limelight.

I felt a bit guilty at first. But, sure enough, began to keep a stock of cat food in the cupboard and welcomed the little thing on my bed. Soft touch, that's me.

He had just turned one year old when he died.

The road between Deb's house and my flat was a busy one. She had popped over to the flat while I was out and Mattie had followed a little way behind as she crossed back towards home, no doubt seeing an opportunity for some extra dinner. It is a constant pain to me that she had to see everything. She saw the car hit him, saw the terrible mess of him as he died in the gutter. Sobbed her fucking guts out as the driver and passers-by came running to try and help. There was nothing to be done of course. He was ruined. The poor love howled and then died, and she saw it all.

My mobile phone had been switched off and I came home that night to a sobbing Debs who told me all about it, the kind neighbour that had carried him back to the house wrapped in a stained sheet and buried him in our back garden.

The boys were also out, watching football with their dad. Debs and I held one another in the kitchen and cried some more, both in sadness at his death and — on my part, certainly — the fact that I hadn't been there.

When Joe and Dan came home there were more tears and Dan and I sat on the sofa in the lounge hugging one another while he talked of 'our' Mattie and how we had shared him.

Nearly broke my fucking heart.

I promised him a couple of days later that I would put Mattie in one of my books and have him be the hero of the story. This meant the world to him. Me too: as a writer it's the best tribute I can give.

So, this is Mattie's book.

Sentimental? Yes. Unashamedly. He was part of our family. Deal with it.

There are two codas to all this: firstly Debs saying that she had always know Mattie would never make 'old bones' – a phrase I'd never heard and the title of the next *Deadbeat* book. Yes, *more* influences.

Secondly, we now have a new Spanish cat (Clive Owens, the extra 's' added for Equity reasons) who is the spit of Mattie in many ways. He may actually be naughtier. I've read the book to him and he seems to like it. Especially the Tuna references.

Life rolls on.

4.

As well as Mattie, there was something of a check-list for this book. Working on the plots for the next six books or so — I haven't been completely idle, you see — I felt the need for Book Two to be just as big and 'rompish' as Book One, but had to widen things a little. I hesitated to introduce 'real' magick (with a 'k', it is a methodology; without that letter, a theatrical entertainment) at so soon a point, but I wanted the landscape to be broader and felt it good to be upfront about these things.

The theme to the 'Deadbeat' series — stylistically anyway — is that of 'no boundaries'. I'm creating a world to play in which has as few limitations as I can bring to it; that is the fun of the thing, after all. This includes stylistic tricks such as those I've played here.

For example, the use of first-person narrative suits these tales, but it can be criticised as letting the reader know that the narrator will survive (not so here: witness Richard Goodwill). I view these narratives as internal dialogue rather than a written journal or some such, and therefore anything goes. 'No boundaries', see?

To add to this, you will note Book Three opens in the third person. It just works better that way.

I owe the 'pre-title' sequence to my editor Ian Alexander Martin who dropped it in to the MS and made me laugh. It can stay; call it a prologue if you prefer!

5.

So, what else do we have?

There's Danny of course. The short story he first appeared in ("Earth" – reproduced here) was originally written under my **Gregory Ashe** pseudonym for an anthology of Christmas stories I put together for a company in California — co-incidentally the same company for whom I wrote *The Organisation* which also introduced Max and Tom.

Having agreed to compile the book, an open call for submissions went out amongst the company's writers and I was swiftly drowned beneath a mountain of sentimentalist short stories. Some were actually fine, but I was disheartened to see how much the festive theme seemed to crank everyone's cliché engines to the max. I had made it clear in the guidelines that what I wanted was something away from the norm; I wanted to cover multiple genres and styles with Christmas as a central theme, but not necessarily as being the driving force.

I couldn't move for fucking orphans and blazing fires.

Eventually, I gathered a slim volume of stuff which mostly worked (a mixture of truly good work and filler in equal measures; I had a deadline to hit and The Boss made it clear that I should lower my expectations in order to 'hit it!'), but no one had written a supernatural story. No one!

So, naturally, I did one myself and slapped good old "Ashe" on the by-line to cover my tracks.

I'm proud of "Earth", actually. I think it works nicely and often regret 'wasting' it on the project in question. I later reproduced it in Humdrumming's first sample book but it fits here as Danny is now well and truly part of the 'Deadbeat' cast list. He will have a book on his own later in the series.

6.

The sound engineer's snoring is cutting into the author's concentration...

"Guess I've waffled on long enough..." he mumbles, reaching for another fag. "Maybe a quick run-down of the 'trivia', then call it a day."

From somewhere a cry of "What isn't trivial about this rubbish of yours?" reaches his ears, but The Author's too busy fighting with his Ronson to note the comment.

7.

Okay... trivial crap:
  a.   I have indeed eaten an entire bag of Fisherman's Friends in one mouthful just as Max proudly announces. Why? Well... because I'm a tit. I came so close to heaving...
  b.   **The Deveraux Pub** where Danny trades was where the **British Fantasy Society** hosted its pre-awards bash in 2006. I got rather drunk there whilst promoting *Makes You Stronger* (which ended-up being short-listed in the end, but **Stuart Young** beat me fair and square with his excellent *The Mask Behind the Face* from **Pendragon Press**... and he beat **Joe Hill** too!). It was a marvellous night getting ripped in the always excellent company of **The Crowther Clan, Mark Morris, Adam Neville** and **Sarah Pinborough**. Hedonists all. I was amongst friends...
  c.   I had a flat in Stratford-upon-Avon which was, just like Max's,

coated with the take-away juice exuded from the kebab shop below. It made things sticky and smelly and I liked it not one bit

d. I loathe *Les Miserables*, and while it would be exaggerating to say that I was actually kicked out for laughing at the kid on the barrier's death scene as Max claims he did, I certainly got told to 'shut up' in no uncertain terms. I couldn't help it! It was the most ludicrously ham nonsense I've ever seen. He 'died' maybe three times, constantly drawing another breath and clutching at his ailing little chest. Some strange people found it touching — there was much blubbering and many tears in my row — but I just couldn't stop giggling. Made no friends that night, I'll tell you.

Enough...

finis.

The author flings his headphones to the floor and goes in search of fresh air and a computer on which to write Book Three.

The technician enters the room after a moment, intending to empty the ash-trays and rid the room of the foetid dank of the last occupant, holding an aerosol tin of air freshener at the ready in order to sanitize the poxie-ridden atmosphere.

But he pauses, then checks that there is no one in the booth as well as ensuring the tape is no longer running.

Suddenly he grasps the microphone in its bracket and launches into a rendition of "The Girl from Ipanema"... as we fade to black... quickly, oh yes...

Special Features:
THE DEADBEAT MARTINI

Greetings fellow indulgers in the joys of grape and grain! Our select cocktail of choice comes this time from none other than our own **Ian Alexander Martin**, editor, Canadian and resolute piss-head. Upon reading the first volume in this delicious series he set to creating a Martini of his very own to wash the taste away. We present it here with drunken familiarity and a reassurance that *'you're our besht friend you are, we bloody love you...'*

THE DEADBEAT MARTINI

After extensive testing, this drink is now available for public release, and open for comments & feedback.

- 3 ounces of vodka
- 1 ounce of Bols® melon liquor
- 1 ounce Rose's® Lime Cordial (note: not lime juice)
- 1 ounce Cointreau® or Triple Sec®

Mix ingredients in shaker with ice; invert end-over-end until it's too cold to hold onto any more; strain into Martini glass; serve with lime wedge to your favourite un-dead, crime-busting individual.

Guy Adams collects careers like baseball cards. In his, surprisingly limited, time he has tried his hand at Museum Curator, Tour Guide, Historical Researcher, Newsagent...

His main occupations however have always been acting and writing. In the former he has mugged people in *Emmerdale*, watched Rugby in *Where the Heart is*, perved around in his y-fronts simulating sex with a woman dressed as a horse (**Genet's** *The Balcony*) and earned something of a reputation by impersonating real people (**Hemingway, George Bernard Shaw** and **Hitler** to name but a few). He also toured as one half of the wittily titled **Adams & Jarrett** on the comedy circuit and is the youngest actor to portray **Sir Arthur Conan Doyle's** Sherlock Holmes professionally.

As a writer, he has churned out scripts for the above comedy shows and falsified Elizabethan Mummer's Plays. A couple of novels, *More Than This* and *The Imagineer* have earned nothing but people seem to like them so he doesn't let it worry him. He is the author of three books about the television series *Life On Mars* — two for **Simon and Schuster** and one for **Transworld**. If nothing else, these have kept him in Gin.

He is currently working on a big book about Sherlock Holmes, a *Deadbeat* novella or three and a children's book set in his adoptive country of Spain which he is rather hopeful that one of the previous mentioned publishers will pay him good money for.

www.guy-adams.com
www.humdrumming.co.uk

OTHER HUMDRUMMING TITLES BY GUY ADAMS:

ALSO AVAILABLE:

Have things become a bit monotonous 'round your way…?

TRY **HUMDRUMMING** INSTEAD!!

ALL YOUR GODS ARE DEAD
By Gary McMahon

ISBN: 978-1-905532-40-7

Can you see <u>all</u> the colours of pain?

Who is sending Doug Hunter mysterious e-mails that
seem to be from his murdered brother, Andy?

Why are severed human body parts being discovered
in drains and rivers across the country?

What is the real meaning behind the graffiti that
ominously states "All your gods are dead"?

When Doug travels to Leeds, where six months ago
his brother's defiled and mutilated corpse was found
on an abandoned industrial estate, he is drawn into
a web of religious mania, orchestrated torture, and deceit.

There he encounters the Church of All Sufferance,
a strange sect comprising of bald, androgynous
men and women who claim that they are able
to see "all the colours of pain".

Then, when he meets and reluctantly starts a relationship
with Andy's ex-girlfriend, all the pieces of a bizarre
cosmic puzzle begin to slot into place, and Doug realises
that the bloodied acolytes who call themselves the Sufferers
have dark and monstrous plans for the entire world...

*All Your Gods Are Dead comes with my highest recommendation
for anyone who wants to read the best new fiction the horror
genre has to offer.*
— **Joe Kroeger**; *Horror World*

A new novella by Gary McMahon,
with an introduction by author Mark Samuels.

TOADY
BY MARK MORRIS

ISBN 978-1-905532-39-1

Welcome to the Horror Club:
a world of werewolves and poltergeists, psychopaths and
shape changers, the unquiet and the living dead.

A fantasy world, of course, for Richard, Robin and Nigel,
the club's members, are ordinary boys from ordinary
families, who just happen to share a taste for the macabre
in films and videos, books and comics. And then they
admit a fourth member to their club — Toady, a far from
ordinary boy with a taste for the macabre in real life. From
the moment he lures the others into a nerve-jangling seance
in a house with a chilling reputation, their lives are blighted
by worse horror
than they have ever imagined.

In a fusion of nightmare and reality, terror stalks the
familiar streets of a sleepy seaside town and waits to
invade the safest home. The pervasive stain of evil spreads
like ripples on a pond, leaving a trail of sacrilege and death
in its wake. One by one the members of the Horror Club are
overcome and forced into a netherworld, halfway between
illusion and reality. It is up to the final member to fight
alone against the evil they have unleashed — until, in the
final battle,
he is joined by an unexpected ally…

Toady is a staggering achievement.
BFS Award-nominated author **Mark Morris** takes all
the established horror conventions and reworks them in a
way
that is completely fresh and inimitably his own,
in this; his first novel.

Like the missing link between **Stephen King**'*s* It *and a post-*
watershed Grange Hill, *Morris' reprinted début novel is a*
blood-flecked snow-storm that will wrap itself around the
reader and carry them into a winter of terrifying discontent.
… Read it in the summer to cool you down like literary ice
cream or during the winter months to listen to the chilly
howling wind outside as you read by bedside light, but just
read it.
– Stuart Weightman; *Starburst Magazine*

WORLD WIDE WEB
— & OTHER LOVECRAFTIAN DOWNLOADS —
BY GARY FRY

ISBN: 978-1-905532-40-7

H.P. Lovecraft isn't dead. He survives. From parody to pastiche, from homage to quite deliberate attempts to deny his influence, modern horror writers have wrestled unspeakably with the master for years. In this collection of Lovecraftian tales, **Gary Fry** takes the un-dead writer to task in a sequence of pieces which explores everything that can be done with his fiction.

Here you'll see how the Mythos can be used to inform contemporary concerns, to provoke laughter, to make you think, to employ alternative narrative devices, to be experimental, and more.

One novella and six short stories, including an introduction by Mark Morris and an afterword from the author.

Cosmic terror awaits you; indifference is not a choice you can make. Read this book and shudder as the dreadful entities gather and the world grows dim and dangerous...

Gary Fry has been behind some of the most sophisticated — and scary — work of recent years, and this superlative collection is no exception.

This is a writer with important things to say and the talent to make them compelling.
— **Melanie Tem**

...powerful ideas that resonate with me.
— **Adam L G Nevill**

The prose is so polished and vivid, and the suspense maintained so powerfully and adroitly...
— **Russell Blackwood**

Fry's writing is assured... effortlessly drawing the reader in to the story and making him care about the characters.
— **Peter Tennant; The Third Alternative**

...powerful ...with many effective and imaginative touches.
— **Ramsey Campbell**

YOU ARE THE FLY
— TALES OF REDEMPTION & DISTRESS —
BY JAMES COOPER

ISBN 978-1-905532-34-6

*You live in a world darkened by the threat of global terrorism, where
the very worst of human nature can be seen in the faces of young and old alike.*

*You walk the streets and sense their fear. They are not just afraid of you;
they are afraid of everything. The married couple whose relationship is
falling apart. The next-door neighbour who furtively stares across the fence.
The street children you once used to know.*

*This is the dawning of a new dark age. An apocalyptic vision of life in
the 21st Century, when only the horror of what you've become remains.*

You are touched by it, and you are transformed.

Your journey has already begun.

You Are the Fly (Tales of Redemption & Distress):
14 subversive stories that illuminate the human condition and
escort you to the very brink of the unknown.

Only those of you who endure shall be redeemed.

With an introduction by **Greg F. Gifune**

The first collection from the prodigious talent of **James Cooper**, whose
stories have already garnered some phenomenal devotion:

*Though James Cooper's love of the traditional horror tale is evident in his writing,
his fiction is anything but formulaic. His work is thought-provoking, passionate,
slightly offbeat, and delves as deeply into the often very real horror of the human
condition as it does elements of the fantastic. A fresh new voice in dark fiction,
James Cooper is a writer on the rise, and deservedly so.*
— **Greg F. Gifune**, author of *Dominion & Deep Night*

"The Other Son" is excellent… in a different league…

— **Graham Joyce**

*Sometimes an unknown writer comes along whose work stuns you. James Cooper
is an original voice in fantasy/horror, a new author who possesses not only a
powerful imagination, but one who can tell a story that really grips the reader
socially, morally and politically and refuses to let go.*

— **Sean Wright**

THE IMAGINEER
BY GREGORY ASHE

ISBN 978-1-905532-00-1 — SNOWSCAPE EDITION
ISBN 978-1-905532-01-8 — FIRE EYE EDITION

If it were that easy, we'd all be heroes

This is not it. The world you know — normal, safe, boring — is just
a stepping stone to other worlds, other places.
Places of magic, monsters and limitless imagination.

Like most eleven-year-olds, Charlie Whittaker
always hoped this was true.

Now he knows it is.

Because somebody's kidnapped his Uncle
and he's forced to give chase.

Leaving normality far behind…

He will make friends on the way: the enigmatic Lashram,
the absurd Squintillion, the noble Algernon. He will see
sights that will make the wildest dreams of his life seem bland.

But will he survive long enough to enjoy them? There are
horrors out there, ravenous cannibals, lethal assassins and,
of course The High Lord Jethryk — a man who wears shadows
torn from his victims and could snuff out all life in the universe
using no more than his smooth fingertips. There is, in fact, only
one power Jethryk doesn't possess, a power he intends to
steal from Charlie's uncle.

By whatever means necessary.

An absolute delight that knocks spots off Harry Potter,
The Imagineer *is a real quality read… The book is littered with
beautiful illustrations… Young adults and mature readers have a
new boy hero, and he's called 'Charlie Whittaker'.*
— DarkSide Magazine

MORE THAN THIS
BY GUY ADAMS

ISBN 978-1-905532-05-6

There was something in the water

Kiss me quick and squeeze me slow, there's something
amiss in the crumbling seaside resort of Gravestown:
Children are vanishing and nobody can understand how.

Gregory Ashe watches them go, sees them hanging from their
tatty 'wanted' pictures and the wilting bouquets of flowers left by
well-wishers. He feels it's nothing to do with him, he's far too busy
with his face in a book and a head full of dreams.

Then, amongst the seaweed and shingle, a solitary foot
is washed-up and the violence begins.

Gravestown is infected. People are beginning to lose their minds,
changing, becoming other. Blood is spilt, over and over and over...

Through it all the waves roll and, in the dark building on the
cliff tops, the lunatics howl by the light of their moon.

Slowly the safe walls of reality are crumbling
and it seems nobody can stop it.

Nobody that is except The Magician, a man who takes young
Gregory under his wing and shows him how hollow those dreams
of his really are, a man with more than just spare decks of cards
hidden up his sleeve.

Gregory's never been in so much danger...

A dark fantasy laced with humour and terror. *More
Than This* is a fast-paced journey from innocence to
maturity, fear to hope, heaven to hell. Exciting, horrifying
and filled with the sort of imagination, escapism and,
above all, magic you remember from books you read
as a child — magic you thought lost.

If you are interested in purchasing any of our titles for yourself or others (and thereby demonstrating your superior intellect and discernment), please direct the attention of your web-browser to the address below.

We thank you kindly in advance for supporting these fine writers and their works.

http://humdumming.co.uk